Torment

Dark Wolves Series book 1

By

Élianne Adams

Cover Art by Jacqueline Sweet Design

Paperback ISBN 9781988644035

Other Titles by Élianne Adams

Return to Avalore Series
Flickering Light
Call of the Dragon
Rise of the Phoenix
Once Upon a Fiery Christmas
Lost in Magic

Dragon Blood Series
Releasing Her Dragon
Her Gingerbread Dragon
Finding His Dragon
His Secret Dragon
Saving His Dragon
Keeping His Dragon (Fall 2017)

Dark Wolves Series
Torment
Betrayal
Wrath
Burden

Sugar Shack Series
Northern Sass
Candy Sass (November 2017)

Deadly Whispers Series
Bump in the Night
Fallen Angel

Single Titles
Black Velvet
Burn Deep

Coming Soon!

Mates of the Citadel Series
Damon (Fall 2017)
Axton
Keilon

Torment

Elianne Adams

http://elianneadams.com/

TORMENT · 2

« CHAPTER 1 »

Darkness. He couldn't escape it. Oh, the day was bright, and the sun's rays warmed his skin, but there was no peace. Not for him. Khet took a deep breath, hoping for... what? He didn't even know. To have the coldness removed from his soul? Maybe he wasn't meant to find the freedom his pack brothers had. Maybe he had escaped the Erritrol curse because of the good men around him rather than his own worthiness.

The shimmering portal, not twenty feet ahead, beckoned him. He could go back. Find his place in the Dark Lands again. Alone. It would be better than risking the others with the evil seeping into him every fucking day. But even though he'd come to that very same spot each day for the past week, he still couldn't make himself cross into the bleakness awaiting him. Each time he tried, the beast inside him snarled and spat, proving how volatile he was even in this place of relative tranquility.

Swallowing his growl, he sat at the base of the tree, the same tree he'd rested beneath every day for the past week. Pine needles pricked at his naked ass, but he didn't shift back to his wolf. He needed the sun's warmth if only to give him the illusion that he might not turn into the monster clamoring to overtake him.

The kaleidoscope of colors swirling in the portal made his head pound. Only in the last few months had he been able to see color at all. Bright yellows and reds were the worst, but he couldn't tear his gaze from the mesmerizing sight. For too long, nothing but blacks and shades of gray had filled his vision, and now he didn't want to miss any of it, even if it made him want to gouge his eyes.

When Argram had insisted they learn the human names for the colors and to differentiate them all, Khet had been the first in line. Hell, he was even teaching himself to read with the human children's books his leader had provided, but maybe it wasn't worth it. Fitting into the human world would never happen. Not for him. Not with the taint on his soul threatening to swallow him whole with every breath he took. It was too risky. He wouldn't give the beast the opportunity to destroy the land and the people in the neighboring villages.

The burn in his gut throbbed like a living fiery pulse, scorching his insides until he could do nothing more than grunt and close his eyes as he let it wash over him. Some days it lasted moments, others hours. Each time, it took his breath and drew the monster closer to the surface.

Off to his right, a twig snapped. He didn't bother opening his eyes. The sound was too light to be human, and very few animals would come anywhere near him. Even their mightiest beast would not be a threat to one of his kind. Erritrols were predators. *He* was a predator. The creature residing inside him assured it.

Had he shifted back to his wolf form, he'd have been able to determine the species by scent alone, but in his humanoid form, he was almost nose blind. And it was irritating as hell. The muscles in his stomach clenched tight then released. He took a long, slow breath, ignoring the pain. Wishing it away accomplished nothing. Maybe that was his punishment for having survived the change. Sweat beaded on his skin, making goosebumps rise on his damp flesh where the cool breeze drifted past. *His skin.* He still couldn't believe he had skin. A year ago he'd been nothing but fur, fangs, claws, fury, and hatred. An Erritrol.

No one knew how close he'd come to succumbing to the evil lurking inside. How close he'd come to doing the unthinkable and harming Brienne, the Avalorian woman who had sacrificed her happiness to help his people. When the curse keeping them from shifting for centuries was broken, he had expected to perish with those who had taken that final leap into madness, yet somehow, he'd been saved. He shook his head and gazed into the portal linking the Dark Lands to the human world. No one knew how hard the darkness still beckoned him, and how easy it would be for him to lose himself in it.

Only once the cramps subsided and he was able to breathe again did he get up from his spot beneath the tree. He took one look at the portal and turned away. He could hold the beast back for one more day. For now, he had won the battle. If the beast came too close to overcoming his will tomorrow, he would go back to his native land and let the darkness take him—let the monster destroy what little of him was left and be done with it. At least there, no innocents would be harmed.

In wolf form, he could be back at camp in no time, but he was in no rush. The sun was still high in the sky, but even if it wasn't, the night held no challenge. He could see as well on a moonless night as he could on the brightest day. If anything, it was easier for him to be out after twilight. Most of the creatures that tempted him beyond reason were bunked down for the night, making his need to kill and destroy less—just less.

A sweet scent wafted to him on the breeze, then as quickly, it was gone, leaving him wondering if it had been there at all. It didn't smell like any of the flowers he'd encountered, but then, he didn't go around sniffing flowers. He could have easily missed some. Inside, the beast stretched and lifted its head. Had it sensed prey? His skin prickled with the fur trying to emerge from his pores, and sweat dampened his brow. Maybe he should give in and let the beast take over. It would be better than the agony of keeping it under control. He growled, more so at himself than at the beast inside him. No, damn it. He wouldn't do it. He wouldn't give in.

He took one step, then another, heading back for camp. A woman's high-pitched scream had him stumbling to a stop at the base of a steep knoll. He didn't move, didn't even breathe as he took in the sounds of the rushing footsteps as they hurtled toward him.

Brush rustled in her wake. Her panting breaths became louder as she neared, but her footsteps didn't falter. Roots and jagged rocks littered the ground. She was going to kill herself if she came crashing down the hill. Not that it mattered to him. It was up to the woman to be aware of her surroundings, yet he stayed there, waiting, his whole body tense.

The same sweet scent that had teased him earlier came back, filling his nose, rousing the wolf. Before he had a chance to beat it back, a small form hurtled from the top of the knoll, her arms flailing when the ground failed to come up to meet her feet as she'd lunged ahead.

Her eyes grew wide, as she fell, slamming right into him.

« CHAPTER 2 »

Delana raced through the forest. Her simple mission to get to the new wolf pack and request their aid had gone sour fast. The Mahehkan pack was close—too close. If she couldn't convince the new wolves to join forces with them, the Komoro pack would suffer the same fate their neighbors had over a year ago. The Mahehkan wolves had slaughtered them in cold blood. Rumor had it one she-wolf had survived the attack, but no one had seen her since.

Her lungs burned with the need for more air. She wished she could have taken the time to remove her clothes and shift, but she'd spotted two wolves pacing her in the forest. She couldn't afford those precious seconds. They would be on her before she could get her shoes off. So she had bolted, running through the forest like an idiot, hoping her knowledge of the land would help her escape. Thankfully, she was fast in either of her forms.

The rocky drop-off ahead was a risk. If she didn't land just right, she'd do some serious damage, but it was her only option. If she could make it there, she could duck left and be out of there before they realized where she'd gone. She'd have to go back to her pack without the extra help they needed, but at least they'd be warned the enemy was coming. Pumping her arms, she forced her body faster. Just a little farther.

One huge leap and she was in the air. Relief flooded her, then winked out in an instant. Standing at the base was the biggest male she had ever seen. Not a stitch of clothing covered his massive body. With her arms cartwheeling all around, she tried to stop, but there was no use. She slammed right into the living mountain, the impact of her body on his hard chest knocking the breath out of her.

Arms as thick as her thighs came around her, holding her up when she would have crumpled at his feet. Eyes so dark she could barely discern the pupils stared down at her. His nostrils flared, and his full lips drew into a straight line. The vibration from his chest shook her even before his growl rumbled from his throat. He was pissed.

Crap. She pushed against his chest with all her might, but nothing could have freed her from the beast who had caught her. There was no escape.

He'd either take her back to the Mahehkan pack where they would either kill her or worse, keep her. From the fury burning in those black eyes, she had the feeling she wouldn't be going anywhere.

Digging her heels in, she shoved at the man again. She didn't plead, didn't beg. Doing so would be useless. The Mahehkan weren't compassionate wolves. All they cared about was expanding their territories, and they didn't care who they destroyed in the process.

His eyes narrowed, and his lips parted, revealing long, pointed canines—longer than she'd seen on any wolf. "Stop," he barked at her, his voice deep, authoritative. And damn if she didn't listen. What the hell was wrong with her?

Two wolves came hurtling over the rise. One landed on its feet a short distance away while the other stumbled. The unmistakable snap of bone sounded just before the clumsier of the two yelped and crashed to the ground.

Delana couldn't breathe. She wouldn't be able to help her pack. She'd failed in her mission. Failed her younger brother. Joss wasn't an Alpha, not yet. Given a few years, things might have been different, but they didn't have that kind of time. If they didn't do something—and fast—Joss wouldn't live to grow into his power. None of them would survive. The

Mahehkan shifters had killed her Alpha and left them without a leader. Delana had done her best to help Joss, but now he'd be on his own.

The steel bands of his arms tightened around her, and his lip curled up in a snarl. Her chest hurt with the pounding of her heart, but he wasn't looking at her. His glare was fixed on the wolf still standing. The guttural sound coming from his throat made her quake. The big gray wolf froze where it was and tucked its tail between its legs. The man growled again, and the wolf bolted. The smaller one, who had made a less than graceful landing, whimpered as it struggled to stand. After one more growl from the man, it dragged its lame leg as it scurried away, yelping with each awkward step it took.

The tension in the man's arms loosened, and the rumble in his chest faded until it was gone, but Delana didn't dare move. She hardly breathed. If he wasn't Mahehkan, then he had to be from the new pack. The one she had been sent out to find. The problem was, none of them knew if the new pack was friendly.

When his gaze found her again, she swallowed hard but refused to lower hers. She wasn't Alpha, but she was Joss's representative, and she had to show strength if she was to win them over to her side. "Thank you," she said.

His eyes narrowed, and he took a deep breath before finally releasing her from his grasp. "Why are those wolves chasing you?"

Right to the point. Okay. She could deal with that. "Their pack is trying to gain territory that doesn't belong to them. They've been encroaching on our lands. Killing our people."

He grunted and peered in the direction where the last wolf had scurried off, as though he'd go after it. It couldn't have gotten far with its injuries. When he looked at her again, his face was a blank mask. "Where are your males? Why are they not protecting you?"

Taking a deep breath, she pushed ahead. "Like I said, they've been killing my pack. Cowardly attacks in the dead of night, sometimes using weapons that we have no defense against. We only have a few males left, and they're protecting the other females and young ones. We need your help."

"And your Alpha approved of you leaving the safety of your pack?" His growl rumbled again, not quite as menacing but still enough to have her heart racing.

"No, not really. I didn't give him a choice. I'm a fast runner. I know these woods like the back of my hand. None of the others would have survived."

"Had I not been here, you wouldn't have, either."

Delana tilted her chin and squared her shoulders. "You're right. But I was still the best choice for the mission."

The man looked at her from the top of her head all the way to her sneakered feet and back up again, then snorted. "Come," he finally said once he'd finished his perusal.

The man was huge, and intimidating as hell, but he—and his pack—were their last chance at survival. And if the other males were even a fraction as huge as this man was, they would be formidable allies. She took a step on shaking legs. "Where are we going?"

"I'm taking you to *my* Alpha."

She nodded quickly and looked down, heat creeping up her cheeks. "Do you need a moment to gather your clothes?"

The man's cheeks flushed pink. "My clothes are back at camp. I didn't expect to need them out here."

She couldn't help but grin at the sheepish look on the big man. "You don't. Let's go."

The man turned and walked down the narrow path at the base of the knoll leading him deeper into the forest.

"Wait. I don't even know your name," she said as she hurried to catch up.

He didn't look back and didn't slow down. "I'm Khet."

"I'm Delana," she told him. She didn't usually like to walk behind a man, but she had to admit, doing so had some advantages. Like the view. All that rippling muscle.

He glanced over his shoulder at her, and she ripped her gaze from where it had been, right on his gorgeous ass. His eyebrows shot up before he turned ahead again. He'd caught her ogling. *Damn.*

« CHAPTER 3 »

Khet did his best to ignore the woman walking behind him, but it was no use. And her constant chatter had nothing to do with it. Sure, he was learning a lot about her people and why she needed his pack's help, but that wasn't where his mind was focused. The second she'd leaped from that knoll, pure need had slammed into him—and it had yet to recede. The scent of her fear had driven the wolf inside him mad. He had wanted to tear her enemy to shreds and bathe in their blood. And he would have. Goddess help him, he'd have taken their lives in a heartbeat. The creature inside him would have destroyed what little of his soul he had left. Had it not been for his stronger desire to stay with her and protect her, he would've given chase.

He had to stop thinking about her. Had to keep his mind off how soft her long brown hair had felt against his naked chest when he'd held her. And her plentiful curves. Sure, they were covered in clothing, but nothing could mask the pure feminine form hiding beneath. The path widened less than a quarter mile ahead, and she'd be able to stand next to him. His cock was so damned hard it was painful. Not that he cared if she saw his cock—she'd been staring at his ass for the better part of ten minutes already—but arriving at camp in such a state would be hell. His pack brothers wouldn't let him live it down.

Reaching over, he grabbed a handful of the dark, ripe berries from the bush along the trail.

"What are you doing?" she asked as he brought his hand up to his mouth.

"Taking you to my Alpha," he said as he popped some of the sweet fruit into his mouth and glanced over his shoulder at her.

"Don't eat that," she said, her tone tense.

"Why not?"

"That's a pokeberry plant. The fruit will make you sick. Did you eat those where you came from?"

He looked at the fruit in his palm and dropped them to the ground. He'd been eating those berries since they'd come to the human lands. "No, berries didn't grow there. We ate meat."

"Best to stick to that here until you know what is safe. I'd be happy to help you if you want."

Already, his gut burned from the berries he'd swallowed before she had stopped him. As much as he craved meat fresh from a kill, he couldn't tempt the beast with animal flesh ever again. It made it stronger, more volatile. "Let's worry about helping your pack first, then we'll see about the local vegetation," he said as he started walking again.

His stomach clenched into a tight knot, and sweat beaded on his forehead. At least with the pain ripping through him, he wasn't so focused on his cock. Although he was far from being flaccid, by the time the path widened, his cock wasn't beating at his lower belly with each step he took.

She took one look at his face, and sprinted ahead. He was about to call her back when she crouched low and plucked at a plant.

"Here, chew on this," she said when he reached her.

"What is it?"

"Mint. It'll help with the pain in your stomach."

He looked at her for a moment and took the little green leaf from her outstretched hand, bringing it up to his nose to sniff. It wasn't unpleasant. Delana gave him an encouraging smile, and he popped it into his mouth, for no other reason than to please her. He doubted a little leaf would do much against the agony ripping through him, but she didn't need to know that. "Thank you."

"You're welcome. I learned a lot about the local flora from our old shaman. I suppose I'll be taking over the position of healer now," she said almost absently.

"What happened?" He suspected he already knew, but the more information he could provide Argram with, the better he could plead the case to help Delana. He wouldn't leave her to her own devices, even if Argram denied her the help, but he hoped his pack would stand with him.

"She was killed during the last attack. Our Alpha was mortally wounded, and she was trying to save his life when the Mahehkans found her." Her voice tightened and her eyes shone but she didn't look away.

"So, who leads your pack since your Alpha's death?"

"My brother," she said.

"And he isn't an Alpha." It wasn't so much a question as a request for confirmation of what he already knew. Any Alpha worthy of his status would have ensured Delana's safety above all else, especially if she was the pack's only healer.

"No, but he's the strongest male we have left."

He nodded and started walking again. He had to admire the fact that the wolf had stepped up even though he wasn't the right wolf for the job. "We're almost there."

When they arrived, the deep voices of his pack brothers filled the small encampment, but all hushed as he walked to the center with Delana at his side.

"Where is Miga?" he asked Wesken as the pack's second approached with furrowed brows. Miga was the only female in the pack and the mate of their Alpha. Above all else, Miga and her cub needed to be protected—always.

"They are safe."

"Good. I need to speak with Argram."

"He's with his mate."

Khet nodded. "Then perhaps I can speak with you, Wesken, and you can confer with your brother on my behalf."

Delana wasn't a small girl—not by any stretch of the imagination—but next to the men circling her and Khet, she was petite. Each of them was at least a foot taller than her five-foot-eight, and they were double her width even with her generous curves. Just glancing at them was hard. Each of them made her inner wolf want to lower her eyes to the ground and submit. If none of the males around her were the Alpha, she didn't know what the hell she'd do when she met him. Probably throw herself on the ground and expose her belly. The thought had a nervous snicker bubbling out of her before she could stop it.

Khet glanced her way, then reached over and pulled her closer so that she was no more than an inch away from him. The instant his hand closed on her arm, her nervousness melted away. His stance was clear. He'd protect her, even from his pack if need be.

"Fine. We were about to eat. Put some pants on and join us." With that, the cranky man who had greeted them turned and walked away, expecting them to follow.

"Stay here," he told her, then glared at each of the males in turn before going into a tent a short distance away. The men around her closed the circle again, not blocking her view, but surrounding her, just the same. Khet wasn't gone a minute, but each second had her heart beating faster and her hands shaking a little harder. When he emerged, he wore jeans and a half tucked, black T-shirt that looked like it would tear down the middle if he flexed his chest muscles.

His upper lip came up in a silent snarl, and the men parted, letting him into the circle. The smell of roasting meat wafted through the air as they neared a fire pit, making her stomach grumble. She was starving after her strenuous run in the forest. "That smells delicious," she said, giving the man Khet had named Wesken a tentative smile when they arrived next to the fire.

The man's scowl deepened before he took a seat on a stump, motioning for her and Khet to do the same. "Why do you need our help?"

Before she could sit, Khet pulled one of the logs close to his and waited for her to settle before doing the same.

"I'm Delana, healer for the Komoro pack, and we are under attack. We have been for some time. Unless we have help, we will not survive the next battle." She gave facts. That's what these men would want, not sentiment or speculation. She continued to tell him about the killing of her Alpha and the decimation of their neighbors. When she finished, his face was as unreadable as it had been when she started.

"I'll talk to Argram—after we eat." The man gave Khet a pointed look before reaching over, grabbing a long stick—the meat on it still steaming—and handing it to her.

Khet stiffened, but after a moment's hesitation, took the offering. He held it, looking at it as though it were as poisonous as the berries he'd eaten earlier before pulling off a small piece and popping it into his mouth. Only once he'd chewed and swallowed—all the while looking at the man across from them—did he hold it out to her. "Eat," he told her.

"There's way too much there for me to eat. Maybe we can share it?" she suggested. Wesken looked at her, his approval evident in his nod.

"There is more than enough meat to fill every belly in this camp. Both of you eat," the man demanded as he took a skewer for himself.

« CHAPTER 4 »

Khet's stomach growled so loudly he was sure every male still circling them—not to mention Delana, who was sitting right next to him—had heard. He hadn't tasted meat, cooked or otherwise, in months. The venison from the young buck his brothers had hunted practically melted in his mouth. As delicious as it was, he wouldn't have another bite. The only reason he had taken that one was to ensure that Wesken would bring the matter of Delana's pack to Argram's attention. The man was stubborn as hell. If he didn't do it, Khet had no doubt Wesken would make good on his unspoken threat.

His suspicion that Wesken knew of his self-imposed starvation was confirmed when Delana had offered to share the food with him, and the man had given her a small approving nod. Wesken didn't approve of anything. Ever. Not since Kendra's betrayal. Maybe even before that.

Already the beast inside him was howling, pushing him for more. Demanding fresh blood and tender flesh. Delana blinked her big brown eyes at him, and he wanted to growl. She pulled off a generous portion of meat, then held out the rest for him to take. He took a slow breath, then another. He swallowed hard and licked his lips, but he didn't reach for the skewer.

She needed his help—his pack's help—but what good would he be to her if the madness overtook him?

Her eyes widened, and she pulled the meat back. "Are you still sick? I can get you more mint. I saw some not far from the camp."

Khet released his breath and shook his head. "I'm sure I will be fine soon. If it worsens, I will get more leaves."

"You are unwell?" Wesken's eyes narrowed.

"He ate some pokeberries along the trail. Those are poisonous to our kind," Delana informed him.

"Pokeberries?"

"Yes, they're those dark berries that grow in clusters off bright pink stalks. The mint leaves help ease it, but I don't imagine it will take the pain away entirely. Until he digests the berries, Khet will have some discomfort. Perhaps we can keep some of the meat for him to eat later?"

Wesken looked at him for a moment, then nodded. "Fine. If you assure me you will get him to eat it, then I will bring your case to our Alpha."

Delana looked him in the eye and nodded. "I'll make sure he eats."

Knowing that Wesken would expect her to keep her word, Khet finally did groan. Her sharp glance and the fact that Wesken had agreed to speak with Argram was all that kept him from protesting. He wouldn't risk changing Wesken's mind.

"I'll see what I can do," the pack's second grunted before leaving the fire, heading in the direction of the Alpha's tent.

They waited by the fire until all the males had eaten and had gone off, still Wesken didn't return. With each passing minute, his frustration and impatience grew. He should have walked into Argram's tent and demanded to speak with him. It wasn't like Delana was a threat to any of them. Of course, the Alpha wouldn't know that, and as powerful as he was, Khet was no match for Argram. If the man saw Delana as a threat to his mate and their cub, there would be nothing he could have done to prevent him from eliminating her.

"So, why aren't you eating meat?" Delana asked in a hushed tone, ripping him out of his thoughts.

He whipped his head around, looking to see if anyone was near enough to hear. "My stomach is cramped." It hurt, but not nearly as much as it had before he'd taken that tiny leaf. And certainly not enough to keep him from eating.

"You only ate a couple of berries, and you had the mint leaf soon after. So I ask again, why aren't you eating meat?"

Before he could answer, Argram and Wesken came into the clearing. Khet stood to greet them. "Argram," he said as he averted his gaze.

Delana stood next to him but didn't say a word. The faint metallic scent of her fear drifted to his nostrils, and he had to fight from making himself a barrier between her and his leader. Argram would want to meet her to determine if she was a threat. Getting in the way would not help her cause.

Khet glanced at her, but her eyes were trained on the ground. A ruby red line blossomed on her bottom lip where she'd pulled it between her teeth and bitten a little too hard.

"Delana of the Komoro pack. Khet. Let's sit and discuss the issue Wesken has brought to my attention."

Khet released the breath he'd been holding and looked up. Argram waited until they were all seated again before starting. "Wesken tells me you are in need of help. Tell me, Komoro wolf, why should we help you? The war between the area wolf packs is not our concern."

Khet wanted to argue, but he couldn't. Delana and her people were not the concern of the Erritrols, but something inside him wouldn't let her suffer at the hands of the Mahehkan pack.

"Well, for one thing, you're on Komoro land. There may be little we can do at this point to remove you from it, but I hope that honor will guide you in making this decision. We've allowed your pack to remain and to hunt in our territory for several months without asking for anything in return."

Argram grunted. "You realize we could easily take this land from you."

"Yes, but since you've not done it yet, I suspect your intention is not to force us from our ancestral homes. And, as lovely as your camp is, we have a village. Actual homes to live in instead of tents. Running water. Electricity. Once winter comes, you would be more comfortable in our village. Not to mention the knowledge of the land and its flora that we would gladly share. I'll admit we have limited funds, but we aren't without resources. We are willing to share all that we have in exchange for your protection."

Seconds stretched into minutes as he considered her. Khet wanted to jump up and scream at the man, but Delana sat there, calm as could be, waiting. Even the faint sound of her heartbeat was slow and steady.

Argram looked between him and Delana and pursed his lips. His mouth opened, but then, apparently thinking better of what he'd been about to say, he shut it again. He looked over at Wesken, grunting once. Khet looked at the brothers. The Erritrol primal language was simple. The tone made it a question. Did he agree?

Khet's heart pounded as he waited. If Wesken said no, then Argram would not be in favor. Argram was the Alpha, but he and Wesken were evenly matched. There would be no winner in a challenge between them.

Wesken looked at him once more, then nodded. It was barely there, and he couldn't be sure Delana would have seen it, but Argram did, and that was all that mattered.

"Very well. We leave in the morning. Khet, she is your responsibility until we get to the Komoro village. She is not to leave your sight."

"Understood."

When the brothers stood, he expected them to leave, but Wesken stopped in front of Delana, piercing her with his stare. "Remember your promise to me." With that, they walked away.

« CHAPTER 5 »

"I'd like to walk in the forest before bed if you don't mind," Delana told Khet as she watched the brothers walk away. Whatever Khet was hiding, it wasn't just from her. Until she figured out what that was, she wouldn't press the issue in front of his Alpha. *Her new Alpha.* She didn't doubt for a second that Argram would take over the pack once they got to her village. The sooner the better. Joss didn't want to be in charge. He'd made his stance clear, but he had been their best choice. There would be no challenge for the position. No blood loss. No one back in the Komoro village was in the same arena when it came to power and strength. She could only hope that he was a fair and kind man.

Khet grunted and nodded. She'd have to learn to decipher the guttural sounds if she wanted to make a life with him, and she did. Her wolf had been prancing inside her from the moment she realized he wasn't going to kill her in the forest. She wanted to lick every inch of him in both his forms, and Delana had to agree, it sounded like a wonderful idea. She didn't know if his people had a sense of fated mates. Not all wolf shifters did. The Komoro pack and their ancestors were lucky enough to have that intuition. And for her, he was it. He, on the other hand, might need convincing.

They walked in silence for a few minutes until she found what she was looking for—blueberry bushes. "These are blueberries. They are safe to eat. A month ago, the berries were green and inedible, but they're plump and ripe now." *A great treat for a wolf who isn't eating meat,* she added to herself. Khet just looked at her. She shrugged and sat, crossing her legs, then popped one into her mouth and smiled before handing him the small handful she'd taken from the plant.

He took one little berry and chewed it, his eyes widening at the flavor. "That's much better than the pokeberry. Thank you." He ate the rest in one mouthful before reaching for more. It wasn't long before the bush was empty. He looked so disappointed that she had to smile.

"Come on." She stood and headed south. The sky was sinking lower, and soon they wouldn't be able to see much of anything. The few handfuls of berries would never fill a male shifter.

They walked a while longer. "Ohhh, wild raspberries. The bushes are prickly and can sting if your skin scrapes against them, but the fruit is delicious."

She picked a few berries and waited for him to do the same. Once he had a taste of them, he kept going. How he maintained his massive body on what he was eating was beyond her. It would never last, though. The James Bay Coast was known for its harsh winter, and wolves survived on meat. She would show him the grove of wild walnut trees so he could eat some protein, but even if he could gather enough of them to fill his belly, he was a wolf, not a squirrel. He couldn't live on berries and nuts forever. It wasn't sustainable—or healthy.

By the time he'd had his fill, and they'd returned to his camp, the sun was sinking past the treeline, and shadows grew longer. Nothing stirred, but she had a feeling the men were watching. It was in the way they'd hung around until Wesken and Argram had come out again that told her they were on guard. But from what? The Mahehkan pack was strong, but she suspected it wouldn't stand a chance against these powerful men.

"I'm sorry that I don't have a nicer place for you to stay," Khet said when he led her to a small tent. The tipi structure looked big enough to hold his human form but not much more. "It's not very big. I usually don't have guests."

Delana smiled up at him. "We can shift if you want. It would give us more room to stretch. I love sleeping as a wolf." Just the idea of snuggling up to him for the night had her wolf wagging her tail and panting. She got a goofy image of her inner beast with her tongue lolling out the side of her mouth, a happy expression on her face, and it was all she could do to keep from laughing.

"No," he said a bit too sharply. "I'd rather stay this way."

So engrossed in having found her mate and looking forward to spending the night so close to him, she hadn't even considered he might not feel the same way. He hadn't asked to have a tent mate for the night, and he sure as hell hadn't asked for it to be her. For all she knew, he had a female in mind already and wouldn't want to be saddled with her.

Her heart sank more than a little. As much as she wanted to explore and enjoy her new mate, she wouldn't push herself on him. "You know, maybe it would be better if I stayed somewhere else. I could go into the forest and come back in the morning—"

"No," he bit out again. "I am tasked with your safety until we reach your village tomorrow. I do not take that lightly. I must insist that you stay with me."

"Let's be honest here. You were told to keep an eye on me to make sure I'm not a threat to your people. It's plain to see I wouldn't stand a chance against a single one of you, much less your entire pack. What harm could come of me going out of the camp and returning at dawn? Your Alpha wouldn't even know I had left."

"He would know. Besides, the Mahenkan pack could be lying in wait. No, you must stay here. The question is, are you willing to jeopardize our agreement by disobeying Argram's order?"

"No, of course not."

"It's settled then."

She waited for him to say more, but he remained silent, his jaw clenched, as he reached for the tent flap, pulling it back for her to enter. As soon as he did, the scent of succulent meat drifted from inside. Almost instantly, he gasped, and his stomach growled.

"Fucking Wesken," he grumbled under his breath as she ducked her head and slipped inside.

« CHAPTER 6 »

"You have to eat more than berries, Khet. It's unhealthy. Your energy will drop, and you will lose strength. What will you do when the berry season is over? When winter hits, you won't be able to eat the fruit, and nuts won't be enough, either," she told him.

With her eyebrows raised and her annoyance crackling like fire in her eyes, she looked more adorable than threatening, but he kept a straight face. Even he knew not to irk a female who was already upset.

"I'll deal with that when the time comes."

A small growl rumbled in her chest. "And what am I supposed to tell Wesken tomorrow? He'll ask me if you ate. I won't be able to lie to him. And then what happens to our agreement? My people will suffer for your stubbornness."

"You'll tell him that I did eat. And I did. You ensured it on our walk."

"And you don't think he'll check to see if the meat is gone? I get the impression that he isn't one to leave anything to chance," she sighed and grabbed the meat from where it leaned on the side of the tent.

Saliva pooled in his mouth, but he wouldn't tempt the beast no matter how much it made his heart ache to see the disapproval in her eyes. Delana pulled a piece of meat from the skewer and took a bite, then another. Each one took longer and longer to chew and swallow as her belly filled, but still, she kept going. She was going to make herself sick by trying to eat enough to make it look like he'd eaten.

"Stop," he told her.

"Will you eat it?"

"No."

"Then I can't," she said as she glared at him. For such a tiny thing, she was awfully brave.

When she tried to force another piece into her mouth, Wesken growled. She paused with the food partway to her lips. He reached over, grabbed the stick from her hands, and stood without a word. Flinging the tent flap open, Khet crossed over to the dying fire. He didn't have to look to know that Delana followed. Her energy sizzled against his skin.

"What are you doing?" she whispered loud enough for any Erritrol to hear.

"I'm stopping you from hurting yourself." He tossed the meat into the smoldering coals, sending sparks shooting up into the air.

Fury shone in her eyes when he turned to face her, but shock, then resignation chased it away when she spotted Wesken coming toward them.

"How much of that did he eat?" Wesken went straight for Delana, not bothering to ask him.

She took a deep breath and dropped her gaze to the ground at her feet. "None."

Seeing her submit to Wesken had Khet clenching his fists and clamping his teeth so hard his jaw hurt.

"You gave me your word, little wolf."

Delana's hand shook as she pushed her hair over her shoulder. "I'm sorry. I failed."

Khet couldn't keep the growl vibrating in his chest contained, earning him a surprised look from Wesken. "She told you she would have me eat, and she did. She kept her word."

He didn't think Wesken would renege on the offer to help Delana's pack, but he wouldn't take chances. He'd go straight to Argram if need be. Hell, he'd go to his Alpha's mate, Miga, and plead his case with her if he had to. And if they still refused, he'd go with Delana and try to protect them himself.

"She is your mate?" Wesken asked in the ancient Erritrol language, his gaze drifting from him to Delana and back again.

"I believe so," he coughed and grunted back at him. Though for the life of him, he didn't want her to be. With his lack of control over his inner beast, the safest thing would be for her to stay as far away from him as possible. Hell, he shouldn't even be considering going to her village at all, but if she *was* his mate, what choice did he have?

Wesken sighed. "Get some sleep. We leave early in the morning," he said in English so Delana would understand before he turned and headed for the treeline.

"I thought for sure he was going to change his mind and not help us," Delana finally whispered when Wesken was out of sight.

"The brothers are intimidating, but they are fair. Come, it's getting late. Tomorrow will be a grueling day," he told her as he led her back to the tent.

Delana lay there, the sounds of Khet's deep breaths teasing her ears. Heat radiated from his body, warming the entire tent, making his scent all the more potent. Every breath she took had her body pulsing with need. Her nipples puckered beneath her shirt and, more than ever, she wished she could be in her wolf form—if only to hide her body's reactions. But then her desire to snuggle closer would be worse. Khet had to smell her arousal, yet he stayed as far away from her as he could. She wouldn't embarrass either of them by making unwelcome advances.

She couldn't even blame him for not wanting to shift to sleep with her. Wolves often liked to snuggle in their lupine forms, but usually only with family or people they considered pack. And they had just met. If her heart ached because he was her mate and didn't feel the same need for closeness, she would get over it. There would be time to win him over once they got to the village. She shifted her weight and closed her eyes. She didn't know how many supplies they would want to carry with them, but she would do her best to help.

She shifted to a more comfortable position on the hard ground and closed her eyes. Morning would come soon enough, and she needed the rest. Tension melted from her body at the soothing sound of

Khet's deep breaths. *If anyone can help my pack, these men can*, she thought as she dozed off.

Delana's heart raced, and she struggled to get enough air into her lungs to ease their burning as she raced from her house into the cool night air. It couldn't be happening. Not again. Vicious growls and the sounds of wolves fighting filled the sleepy village. She rushed to the pack house and nearly stumbled at the sight of the bodies strewn all over. Some were the enemy. Too many were Komoro. To her right, Joss battled a huge gray wolf. Both had blood dripping from various injuries. She rushed forward, though what she would do against such a strong enemy, she had no idea.

"Go to Rasha. Lock yourself in. Protect her," her Alpha demanded as he bounded past her. She whimpered as she saw the gray wolf launch itself at her brother. "Go. Now," he commanded, his voice a deep, deadly growl.

"Delana."

Arms of steel clamped around her, and she fought against them, biting and clawing with everything she had. She had to get to Rasha. She was with cub, and she needed protection. She wouldn't let her Alpha down.

"Delana. Stop."

Her arms were wrenched up high above her head, the wolf's body pinning her to the ground. Delana opened her mouth wide, ready to take a bite out of the bastard that was attacking her when another loud growl rumbled all around her.

Delana 's eyes popped open, and for a moment, she didn't know where she was, only that she couldn't move. She bucked up against Khet, trying to free herself.

"Enough, Delana. You're safe," Khet said.

« CHAPTER 7 »

Delana buried her face in Khet's neck. Her breaths came in short, haggard pants, and her whole body shook, making her teeth chatter. A small sob tore from her throat, and he wanted to destroy whatever and whoever had caused her such distress, even if it were only in her dreams. The need to defend—to destroy—pulsed through him like a living, breathing thing. It should have given the beast inside him more power, fueled its fury, but although it was alert, the creature made no move to push to the surface. Khet waited for it to fight his restraint. His breath caught in his throat. A moment passed, then another, yet nothing.

Khet released Delana's arms and tried to roll off her, but she wrapped her arms around him and clung tightly. He should have peeled her off and kept his distance, but the sniffles she tried to hide and the warm trail of her tears against his neck had him wrapping his arms around her and taking her with him when he turned onto his back.

With long, gentle strokes up and down her spine, he held her until her breaths lengthened again and she relaxed against him. He should've moved her, put her back on her side of the tent, but he didn't want to risk waking her. He'd let her sleep for a while, then once he was sure she wouldn't wake, he would set her away from him.

Khet woke to a damp spot on his chest and his cock so hard he could barely think with the ache between his legs. The cool air had goose bumps rising on his damp skin. Was Delana crying again? Had he hurt her while he slept? His heart pounded. He almost didn't dare open his eyes for fear of what he might find. He couldn't smell her blood, but there were many ways to hurt a person without shedding a single drop.

He took a steadying breath. The first thing he saw when he looked down were her big brown eyes, pupils open wide, staring up at him. Her plump lips were poised just over the spot the goose bumps still covered. She had her body half on top of him, pressing her curves into him. Never taking her gaze from his, she bent closer and ran the tip of her tongue over his skin in a long, slow lick.

His moan filled the tent. He should put a stop to it, hell he should get her as far away from him as he could, but he wanted that soft tongue of hers on his body again so badly it hurt. His already full cock throbbed and twitched in his jeans, making them more uncomfortable than they usually were. He held his breath as she continued looking up at him. The corners of her lips tipped up a little, then she licked him again, this time coming dangerously close to his nipple.

She didn't make him wait long before she flicked her tongue over his skin, sliding its velvety surface over his puckered flesh. Khet moaned again and let his head fall back to the ground.

"I didn't mean to wake you," she said, her voice belying her words. "I couldn't help myself. Your scent is driving me mad."

He lifted his head. "We shouldn't." Even as he spoke, his arm tightened around her waist, bringing her closer.

"Why shouldn't we?" She pressed her lips to his chest, then opened them, grazing her teeth on his flesh.

His heart pounded so hard he could barely hear his thoughts. One bite, right there above his heart, and she would claim him. She would mark him as hers for all time. Did she know that? Would she want it?

He took a breath, bringing her scent into his lungs, savoring the smell of her arousal. The beast inside him roused. *Take. Claim. Mate*, it chanted over and over. *Take. Claim. Now.* He tried to shove the gravelly voice from his mind, but nothing would silence it.

She circled his nipple with her tongue, then sucked the tight tip between her lips in a kiss that stole all reason. With a groan, he pulled her up onto his chest before bringing her head down to his. Taking advantage of her surprised gasp, he plundered her mouth. The taste of her exploded his senses, making him desperate for more. If he'd been unsure before, he wasn't now. She was his. No one else would have her. He brought his hands down her back, pressing her closer, plastering her breasts to his chest. Even with the fabric of her shirt still separating them, he groaned at the sensation. He grabbed hold of her hips, pulling her flush against him. She moaned, then with a needy whimper, she shifted pelvis as far as his hands would allow, rubbing herself against him.

Too many clothes. They had to get rid of them. All of them. Now. He grasped the back of her T-shirt with both hands, and with one sharp tug, the material parted. Delana tried to pull away, but he wouldn't let her. He couldn't. The beast wanted more—needed more. He growled as he continued to ravish her mouth.

"Need to get it off," she panted when she managed to pull away from his lips.

Khet cupped her ass with both hands, keeping them connected while she pushed away from him long enough to let the mangled shirt fall from her arms. As soon as the material was removed and she had it tossed to the side, she closed the gap, taking his lips in another searing kiss.

He had to put an end to it, but her mouth was on his, and her hands stroked his neck, shoulders, and arms—wherever she could reach. And he was powerless to stop. The beast had the upper hand.

He flipped her onto her back and covered her body with his own. Her eyes widened, but she didn't struggle. Didn't protest. *Take. Claim. Mate. Now.* The chant grew louder and louder until he could hear nothing else.

Damn it. He wouldn't hurt her. He fought the need to tear the rest of her clothes off. He gentled his kiss, but couldn't quite break it. She burrowed her fingers in his hair, dragging him closer as she arched into him.

She pulled her lips away, turning from his kiss. "Yes, more," she whispered as he wrapped her legs around his waist.

With another moan, he kissed her jaw and down the column of her neck. He didn't stop until he reached one gorgeous breast. He tongued her nipple, flicking it back and forth with the tip of his tongue until she writhed beneath him and thrust her hips up to meet his. He took the hardened peak into his mouth and sucked. She gasped and moaned, tugging at his hair, bringing him closer. *Claim. Mate. Take*, the beast demanded.

When she slipped one hand between them and stroked the bulge of his cock, all thought vanished. He couldn't hold the beast back. Blood pounded through him like a tribal drum, punctuating each word the beast screamed at him. *Mate. Now. Claim. Mate. Now. Take.* Its frenzied litany had him growling and reaching for her jeans. He couldn't slow down. Couldn't stop. There was no denying the beast.

A series of coughs and grunts outside his tent had him stiffening, but he didn't release her nipple. "Wesken will come for you himself if you don't get out of the tent." Orrin, the youngest of their pack, said in the ancient language.

Khet growled, the sound deep and vicious. His arms tightened around Delana, and he thrust his hips against hers again. She wouldn't get away.

Orrin laughed.

The young Erritrol had no sense. Khet would beat the stupidity out of him later.

"It was just a warning. The sun will be up in the sky soon. We've left this one for last, but your tent is next to come down. It's up to you if you want us all to watch."

Delana gasped, and her body stilled beneath his. Orrin had spoken in the human tongue. The young Erritrol's energy faded as he retreated, leaving him alone with Delana again.

"Shit," she whispered against his neck. Then she did the unthinkable. She licked him again.

He braced some of his weight on his elbows and let the tension seep out of his body with each labored breath he drew. It took all his concentration to subdue the beast. Only then did he lift his head from where he'd tucked it next to hers.

"Damn it," he whispered under his breath. It took everything in him to move away from her body. "They won't give us much time. If we don't dress now, the tent will come down around us."

"You're kidding, right?" her eyes grew wide as she heard grunts coming closer to the tent.

"I'm afraid not." Khet rolled to the side, letting her move out from beneath him.

Delana reached for her shirt. "I can't wear this."

He reached behind him and grabbed one of his. "It's going to be big, but you can wear this," he offered. Anything was better than having her standing with his pack brothers with her gorgeous breasts on display.

She had barely whipped it on and tied a knot at the bottom when the tent started coming down.

« CHAPTER 8 »

Birds chirped their happy songs, and the light of dawn shone through the trees when they emerged from the now partial tent. The few men Delana had seen around the camp the day before had already disassembled almost everything in sight. As they worked, more men returned from the forest around them, assuming duties without a word and strapping what they could to their bodies. A dozen or so men carried everything while the rest carried nothing. She hadn't realized there were so many of them.

"Why aren't we all helping? Seems a little unfair to have them carry it all," she said as she reached for a smaller package she might bring with her.

Khet shook his head. "We all have our tasks. They will carry the camp. The rest of us will defend them in the event of an attack."

"There's no way the Mahehkans would be foolish enough to attack you. Your pack is much more powerful. You would decimate them."

"We're not worried about them."

She was about to ask another question when Argram gave a mighty roar, silencing her. The men around her grunted and coughed, but since none moved in a defensive position, she took a breath and waited.

"It's time to leave," Khet told her before he motioned for her to go ahead of him.

Delana—and her wolf—were irritable. They'd come so close to connecting with their mate that morning. Had it not been for Orrin announcing that they would be dismantling the tent around them, Khet would have taken her. Maybe even claimed her. And she had been ready for it. Eager for it. But ever since he'd climbed out of the tent, he'd barely looked at her, much less spoken to her.

But that wasn't all that was annoying her. The faint scent of the Mahehkan wolves clung to the air. At least she didn't see them—and she wouldn't. Not today. The scent was too faint. They had to have retreated after coming face-to-face with Khet the day before. The smart thing for them to do would be to give up and leave them alone, but she doubted that would happen. The Mahehkan wolves were strong, but they weren't that smart.

Even though she was on alert for any movement in the forest around her, Delana's entire body tingled with awareness. She wasn't going out of her way to brush up against Khet, but she wasn't trying to avoid it, either. If he had issues with her nearness—and the tension making his usually smooth walk jerky each time she touched him showed he did—then that was his problem.

Being so close to him with him acting like they hadn't almost torn his tent down with the passion they had shared was killing her. Every part of her wanted to climb the man like a tree and kiss him senseless. It didn't matter to her—or her wolf—that he'd barely said two words to her since they had left the seclusion of his tent. She still wanted him. Oh, it had stung when he had put distance between them, but now wasn't the time to deal with it. Once she had them settled in the village, she would corner him if she had to, and they'd hash it out. Until then, she'd bury her frustration and do what needed doing. And that was to get them to the Komoro village.

She led Khet and the rest of the pack through the forest, happy to be heading home. She had no doubt that they could find her village without her if they wanted to. Hell, they probably had, but still, they let her lead. It probably had more to do with the fact that they were able to keep their eyes on her from their positions behind her than anything else.

Delana had caught a glimpse of one single, stunning female with glorious blond hair among them. Even more noticeably, she carried a toddler with her. The baby had to be somewhere around two from the looks of him. Argram, the Alpha, stood with her, scowling at everyone that came anywhere near them. She hadn't gotten close enough to earn that scowl. No fewer than three of the huge men stood between her and the woman at all times. The rest surrounded the group, cutting through the forest around them to maintain formation even when the brush was thick and the way was difficult.

They were a few miles from the village when a prickle of unease washed over Delana. The sick, oily sensation had her skin burning as though thousands of insects stung her at once. Her stomach lurched, and her head pounded with sudden pressure. She gasped and doubled over, her stomach trying to get rid of its contents.

Khet growled and shoved her behind him.

"What's happening?" She struggled to get air, but it burned her lungs as though filled with smoke, yet the air was clear.

Growls rose all around them as the men closed rank, shoving her into the thick of the men strapped with supplies, the blond woman, and the child. "Get down, and stay down," Khet ordered as he turned to face an unknown enemy.

Delana brushed at her arms, but when she looked, nothing was there. She heard a vicious roar, then another before a brilliant flash of light struck down the path they had been heading.

The child, much closer now, cried as the woman held him close, shushing him with a soft sound. Fear shone in the woman's eyes, and Delana knew she would do anything to protect them from whatever was out there.

Tremors shook the ground beneath her feet, balls of what looked like charged electricity flew in the air. One of the men close to her roared as he whipped his hands before him, forming a circle, then sent a ball of his own out into the forest. But it was too late. A large red orb struck him straight in the chest. The man grunted, then fell to his knees, and in an instant, he was gone. All that lingered was a shower of dust and the smell of burned flesh.

Delana gagged and dropped to the ground. The howls around her had her heart pounding and her whole body shaking. What was that? She scrambled on the ground, getting closer to the woman and child, taking the position the male had occupied. But what the hell was she going to do against a red ball of...whatever the fuck that was?

A massive creature standing on two legs shimmered then appeared not ten feet in front of her. Black, soulless eyes bored into her. Its elongated snout was almost wolf-like, but otherwise, it held no semblance. Long, yellowed teeth protruded from its mouth. Four-inch claws, sharp and pointed, clicked together as it clenched and unclenched its fists.

She wanted to scream, wanted to run, but no way in hell would she leave the mother and child to this beast—this monster. She stood on shaking legs and faced it with her head held high. She could shift to her wolf form—it would take a few seconds to do it since she wasn't nude—but if she timed it just right, she could go for its throat before it had a chance to shoot off anything that sizzled again. She hoped.

Before she could do more than think about shifting, one of the males close to her threw a blast of blue and orange light into the creature. It growled and shook. After a moment, it threw its head back and roared. Spittle sprayed from its mouth. Another shot from the other side of her, landed in the beast's chest, silencing it. Then with a groan, it turned to dust.

Delana looked into the forest, searching for the new threat. And there was one. The growls coming from the men around her told her as much. The whine of whatever they were throwing made her ears ring and her head pound. Argram's mate reached up from behind her, dragging Delana down until she crouched with her and the child.

"You can't fight them. Let the men take care of this," the blond woman yelled over the wicked sounds.

Delana tried to get a glimpse of Khet, but she couldn't see him anywhere. Her heart raced. Had he been incinerated on the spot like the other male had? A small sob lodged itself in her throat, but she refused to let it out. There was no way her mate had perished before they'd gotten to know one another.

She might not have the ability to fight the creatures on their terms, but there was nothing stopping her from being a barrier between the monsters and the child. She hunched her back, digging her fingers into the earth as deafening roars sounded all around and bursts of light flashed above her.

« CHAPTER 9 »

Khet blasted an Erritrol twenty feet to his left. He couldn't see Delana, but he had to trust the men in the inner circle would keep her safe. His job was to eliminate the threat, not to worry about the women, but that didn't stop his mind flicking back to his mate every few seconds.

A rumbling snarl came at him moments before the foul energy hit. The wayward blast caught him in the arm. Had it been a direct hit, he wouldn't have survived. As it was, fiery pain sizzled along each nerve ending, cramping each muscle. He fell to his knees as he forced the energy to dissipate and leech from his body. Khet managed to lift his head just in time to see the enemy approach. This creature wasn't just an Erritrol—it was an Ikabrol, an ancient. They were more powerful and more depraved—more deadly. Pale rings of fur circled its neck and wrists. Khet scrambled to his feet. Standing on two legs, it hovered over him by nearly a foot. Matted brown fur covered its body, but Khet knew the power behind all the fur—the malevolence. He knew it because he lived it. Not all Erritrols escaped the darkness when Brienne had broken the curse. And those that remained had no humanity left at all.

The beast snarled as it kept its gaze locked on him. When the Ikabrol lifted its hand, a small orb of black energy swirled in its palm. Khet groaned. It opened and closed its fingers around it, making it sizzle and pop.

He'd never survive such a hit. Khet leaped to the right, the heat of the energy blistering his ear before striking the tree behind him. The crack of splintering wood and the sweet smoke coming from the broken tree filled the air. The Ikabrol took another step closer, a new weapon already forming in its hand.

A flash of white sprung from the left, driving into the Ikabrol just as it was about to discharge its blast once more. Even with the hit, the beast barely moved, but again, Khet got lucky, and its aim was thrown off. In the time it took the creature to right itself, Khet had gathered what he needed and sent it flying straight and true. Another blast, a larger one, came from behind him, combining their power. The ancient roared and shook its massive head. His form shimmered, and then it was gone. The small wolf that had charged the Ikabrol lay there, panting and shaking, but as far as he could tell, it hadn't come to any harm.

Khet turned around in time to see the last enemy fall. Even though the pain still thrummed through him, he stumbled forward. He had to see her. Had to know she was alright. Each excruciating step had his heart pounding and his knees growing weak. Where the hell was she?

Argram assessed the damage—the casualties—from his place at the center. Miga stood with him with their son cuddled close, soothing the boy with soft words and a tender touch. Wesken was helping the men back to their feet and gathering the supplies the men had discarded to help protect the women—but no Delana.

A deep, burning fury rose from his gut, scorching him from the inside out. His mate. Where the hell was his mate? He whipped his head from one side to the other, needing to find her. The growl that exploded from his throat belonged to the beast. Nothing would stop it from finding her—and short of that, avenging her.

Miga looked at him, her eyes wide, and took a step toward him, but Argram pulled her back. She glared at her mate, thrust their son upon him, then broke free from his grasp. Khet saw her approach. Her lips were moving, but he couldn't hear her over the pounding of his heart and the howling in his mind.

She reached for him, placing her hand on his forearm. All around him, he saw his pack—his men—standing with charged energy aimed at him.

When he continued to growl, Miga rolled her eyes at him and took his hand. Every male froze, waiting, ready. She turned him around and pointed at the white wolf still laying where the ancient had been, shivering and shaking.

Khet's breath caught in his throat. He'd never seen Delana shifted. It didn't seem possible that someone with hair as dark as a raven's feather would have a white pelt. He took a step toward the wolf, then faltered. When Miga smiled at him and nodded, shoving him forward again, he exhaled and moved a step closer. Before he knew it, he was kneeling on the ground beside the little wolf. For a moment, she didn't open her eyes—didn't move—and the fury inside him threatened to swallow him whole, but then her chest rose and fell. And again.

Khet found himself breathing with her, letting the air fill his lungs, willing it to fill hers. When the wolf opened her eyes, he nearly crumbled.

"Can you shift back?" he asked, his voice nothing more than a croak.

The wolf lifted its head and looked at the men behind him.

"I'll give you something to cover you."

The wolf shivered again, and then with a yelp, she transformed. It only took a second, but in that time, agony crossed her beautiful features, making him want to howl. But the moment she had, she collapsed again. He pulled his shirt over his head and quickly slipped it on her before lifting her in his arms.

"We have to get her to her people. Something is wrong," he said as he faced Argram.

"She did her duty well. She protected Miga and Malec. Even after being struck by an Erritrol's blast, she moved on to protect you. Your mate is courageous, as well as strong. She will survive," Argram said as though saying the words would make them true.

"How hard of a blast did she take?" he asked as he held her close. She looked like she was sleeping, but the pulse at her neck was too erratic. Her breaths labored from her lungs. Delana was struggling to live, and there wasn't a damned thing he could do about it. "We have to get her to Brienne. She'll know what to do."

"No, there is no time," Argram said. "She needs rest. She will heal. If she was going to succumb, she would have done so by now. Right now, we must honor her wishes and do what we agreed to do. The Erritrols have found us. The Komoro need our protection more than ever."

Khet heard the words, but they held no comfort. All somber, his brothers stood, waiting. Since they'd had their emotions restored, the death of any of their pack hit each and every one of them hard. Orrin, hunched over a fallen brother, had his fingers fisted in his hair while rumbling growls punctuated his haggard breaths. And he wasn't the only one. Men stood, fists clenched at their sides, guarding their fallen. Waiting for their Alpha. Khet's heart thudded. How many had they lost?

After a moment, Argram threw his head back and howled, not once, not twice, but four times. *Four.* His throat tightened, and pain tore through him. After Argram's last roar died down, he and the rest of the pack joined in, mourning their fallen brethren in the way of their people, honoring them the only way they could.

« CHAPTER 10 »

Delana heard the howls from a distant place. The pain in the sound shredded her soul. She wanted to mourn right along with the pack, but she was too far gone. The darkness had swallowed her whole, but she struggled trying to find a way back. Each time she tried, it kept sucking her in deeper until she saw nothing at all.

The only thing anchoring her to life was the heat of the body pressed so close to hers. The rise and fall of his chest as he took a deep breath and howled again, and again. His body shook as he let the pain wash over him—through him, but he didn't let her go. She snuggled into his heat and stopped struggling against the rest that beckoned her. Khet had her. He would keep her safe.

Delana drifted in and out. She opened her eyes only to squint against the harsh sunlight as they crossed the meadow, but she couldn't stay awake. Just opening her eyes sapped her strength. When she moaned, Khet shifted her in his arms. "Sleep, Muhurua," he whispered.

When she woke again, she tried to take a deep breath, but her lungs wouldn't cooperate. Vaguely aware that she was no longer in Khet's arms, she reached for him. Or at least, she tried, but her arms were as heavy as lead.

Pounding like nothing she'd ever experienced blasted through her mind. Voices she was sure had to be hushed screamed in her ears.

"Like hell, you're going to lay with her," she heard Joss say, his whisper exaggerated in anger.

"I will," Khet replied, just as angrily.

"Get out of my sister's house," Joss wasn't whispering anymore. "We don't need your help that badly."

Delana fought to open her eyes, blinking hard to get rid of the blurriness. She was in her house, in her bed. The men stood at the end of it, both wary, and equally determined. She opened her mouth to speak if only to tell them to shut up before her head exploded, but her throat was so dry she couldn't do more than wheeze a breath past her lips.

"I'm. Not. Going. Anywhere," Khet said, bringing his face to within an inch of Joss's.

Delana licked her lips and swallowed what little saliva she had in her mouth. "Stop." She tried to lift her head from the pillow, but it wouldn't budge.

Joss growled, his lips curling back from his teeth.

"Stop," she said more firmly. It was still a whisper, but louder than before. "Mate."

At this, both men turned and faced her. Khet gasped and came to her side, as did Joss.

Joss looked at her, then at Khet, then back down to her again. "Him?"

All she could do was give him a small nod. She had no energy for anything more.

"She needs water," Khet said as he sat next to her and pulled her to a seated position.

Joss bounded out of the room, only to return a moment later with a tall glass of water. He held on to it for a moment, glaring at Khet, then finally gave in. No matter how much posturing he had been doing— how protective he had been of her—Joss was no match for Khet, and they both knew it.

Khet tipped the glass up to her lips. And if it weren't for the vibration on top of the water, she wouldn't have known he was anything but calm.

"Small sips," he told her.

Even with him controlling how much water she took into her mouth, she coughed and spluttered with the first mouthful. Once her throat wasn't quite so dry, he let her take bigger sips until she was gulping the liquid down. She didn't stop until it was all gone, yet she still wanted more.

"Later," he promised. "Right now, you need sleep."

She would have argued, except that none of her muscles seemed to want to work. She tried bringing her hand up to smooth away worried lines on his brow, but it stayed right where he'd placed it on her lap. "What's wrong with me?" she asked him, her heart racing and fear turning her blood cold.

"Nothing more sleep won't heal." He set her down with her head on the pillow.

"Don't go," she whispered, her eyes becoming blurry again, this time because of the dampness in them.

"I'm not going anywhere."

"Lanie," Joss said from where he was still standing by the bed. "Are you sure that's a good idea? I can stay with you if you don't want to be alone."

"I'm sure." She tried to reassure him, but her eyelids grew heavy, and the sounds around her faded to a dull roar.

"I won't be far if you need anything," by the tone of his voice, Joss's words were more of a warning for Khet than anything.

When Delana woke again, it was to a heavy arm draped over her waist and a hard chest pressed against her back. Khet's scent surrounded her. His heated breath fanned her neck. A full moon shone brightly outside her bedroom window, and for the first time in many months, Delana sighed and drifted back to sleep unafraid.

***

Khet's heart raced at full speed one moment—pounding so hard he was sure the sound would wake Delana—and the next, it beat in a peaceful rhythm that had him drifting into slumber. He tried his best not to sleep, but every once in a while, he'd wake with a start. He would have shifted to a less comfortable position on the bed, but that would have meant disturbing Delana, and he wasn't about to do that. The woman needed the rest. And a safe place inside her home. But how safe could she be when she was lying next to him—a creature just as wicked as the ones they'd destroyed in the forest? If she knew, she never would have invited him or his pack to join hers. And she never would have consented to have him in her bed or named him as her mate.

When she'd uttered the word as she had come to, as soft and breathy as it had been, it had blasted through his mind like a cannon. His knees had almost buckled at the sound of her voice, weak as it was, then again, when his mind registered what she'd said. He had suspected that she might be his, and his reaction when he couldn't find her had confirmed it, but until she had said the word, he had hoped she hadn't been the wiser. It would have made things a lot easier. For him, at least.

Telling a woman he wasn't interested was one thing. Rejecting his mate was another. *Damn it.* If he left now, he could be at the portal before morning. He could be out of her life, taking the beast inside him with him. At least she'd be safer. Argram would not abandon them. Not now. So even if the Erritrols returned, she would have their protection. The problem was, he didn't want to go.

Delana stiffened in his arms. "What's wrong?" She tried to sit up, but she was still too weak, and he held her where she was. From his vantage point behind her, he could see the quick rise and fall of her breasts. Her short, little breaths panted on his arm. She grabbed a hold of his forearm and tried to move it.

"Nothing is wrong, Muhurua," he whispered into her hair.

She ceased her struggle and turned her head toward him, her brows coming down and her eyes flashing. "What did you call me? My name is Delana. You should try to remember it." She huffed and tried to get away from him again.

For a moment, he lay there, stunned, then the realization of what she'd said set in. A bark of laughter erupted from his chest, harsh and rough. It only made her scowl deepen, which in turn made him laugh harder.

"It's not funny," she spat as she wiggled against him, trying to get away. Already her movements slowed as the weakness returned.

"Stop, Muhurua. You will hurt yourself. You're still healing." He tightened his arm around her waist, pulling her flush against him, groaning when the curve of her ass nestled into his crotch.

"Then stop calling me by some other woman's name."

"I did no such thing. Muhurua is a word in my family's native language," he assured her, unable to tolerate the pain lacing her words.

"I thought you spoke in grunts and coughs." She settled, her body melting against him.

He sighed. "We do. The primitive language is well...primitive and simple. Most of our kind understand it. The other is taught in certain packs and tribes. It is not so commonly known. Even in our pack, not all know it. Our Alpha and his brother understand it and speak it, Miga, as well as a few other males do as well, but the rest don't. It is why we use the primitive language to communicate."

"What does it mean?"

Delana wrapped her small hand around his wrist and pulled it higher on her chest, covering part of her breast, bringing his hand to rest above her heart.

"The coughs and grunts mean different things. How we deliver it is just as important as the cough or the sound."

"No. Muhurua. What does Muhurua mean?"

His breath caught in his throat. He should never have used the term. "There is no translation for it," he lied. He couldn't tell her he'd named her "his heart" then turn around and leave. But that was exactly what he had to do.

« CHAPTER 11 »

Khet's body was as taut as a bow behind her. He was lying. Whatever Muhurua meant, he didn't want her to know. Disappointment rushed through her. It was silly. Delana barely knew the man, but he was her mate, and he wasn't honest with her. That hurt a little. If it wasn't a woman's name, then the way he had said it, it had to be an endearment of sorts, and the fact that he wouldn't admit it stung.

He hadn't denied being her mate when she'd woken and named him as such. Nor had he shied away from it. Maybe it was so Joss would leave him with her? But if he cared nothing for her and had no intention of seeing where their mating could lead, then why insist on staying with her at all? Why not go to one of the empty houses to claim one for himself?

She settled deeper into his warmth, needing his closeness even if he didn't need hers. Her whole body ached as though she had gone through weeks of intense physical activity. Whatever had happened out in the forest, even her accelerated wolf healing was struggling to get past it. When she wiggled closer, he gasped and then pulled her tighter before exhaling against her shoulder with a moan.

Maybe what Khet needed was a reminder of some of the finer points of being mated. Like intimacy and pleasure. Pulling his hand from where she'd rested it against her breast, she brought it up to her lips.

"Muhu—Delana, stop," he said, but his voice lacked the conviction it would have needed to keep her from doing what she intended.

Without uttering a word, she popped one of his fingers into her mouth. She swirled her tongue around it and then sucked.

He groaned again and thrust his hips forward, pushing his hard length against her rear.

When she released it, she didn't give him the opportunity to protest. She turned to face him. She still wore his T-shirt. It hung off one shoulder, exposing a generous expanse of her breast. And when the hem caught beneath her hip and pulled the fabric tight across her chest, she didn't try to fix it.

His breaths grew ragged, but he didn't pull away. "We can't do this, Delana."

Her heart sank at the weariness in his eyes. Why? Why couldn't they do it? All of it? He was hers. She was his. There was nothing stopping them from making love or even exchanging the mating bite. Nothing but him. She wanted him more than she'd ever wanted any male. And the bulge pressing into her thigh didn't lie. He wanted her, too.

"We can. Why not see where this leads us if you're not certain? I don't expect a commitment from you right now." Her wolf yearned for more, but she could wait. What choice did it have? If Khet didn't want her as a mate, it was his right to deny her. For her, though, he was it. She wouldn't have another. And if a night or two of passion was all she'd have with him, she wanted it all.

He groaned and closed his eyes. "It's not that simple."

Rather than argue with him, she leaned closer and pressed her lips to his. She didn't push him, didn't make demands. She just stroked her lips across his, breathing him in, etching his essence into her soul. After a moment, when he didn't move, she sighed and pulled back. As much as she wanted him, she wouldn't make a fool of herself. He looked into her eyes until she thought she might have to look away, but then he groaned and pulled her closer again. Bringing his hand up to the back of her head, he held her in place. He swiped his tongue across her bottom lip, then the top. When she opened up to let him in, he moaned and slipped inside.

He closed his eyes as he pulled her flush against him. Her breasts pressed against his hard chest.

"Delana," he whispered on a sigh when he pulled his lips away and trailed kisses down her neck. The heat of his mouth on her body had need pulsing through her. Her nipples puckered, and her clit throbbed. She'd had his lips—his mouth—on her back at his camp. The madness of the moment wasn't the same. It wasn't any less potent, but it was different. If this is what he did to her before he touched her, she couldn't imagine how good it would feel when he got to the areas that needed attention most.

When he reached the neckline of her shirt—his shirt—his impatient growl vibrated from his chest. Before she could even think to move, the shirt was gone, and her bare skin made contact with his. All that separated them were the jeans he still wore.

She didn't have time to worry about how the shirt had disappeared. He brought his mouth down to the valley between her breasts as he slid his entire body lower. When she tried to wiggle to reach the snap of his jeans, he held her in place with a gentle hand on her chest.

"Don't move."

"Are you always this bossy in bed?" she asked, softening the question with a grin. It didn't matter. She loved that he took charge.

A sexy growl, which vibrated straight to her clit, was his only response as he drew her nipple between his lips and sucked. The softness of his tongue around the pebbled tip had her gasping. Over and over he circled it, then flicked the tip before repeating the torture.

Just when she thought she couldn't take any more, he moved to the other breast, using his fingers, teasing the one he'd left. He tugged on her already sensitive bud as he sucked the other between his lips. Arching her back, she pushed herself closer.

"Khet, please," she begged.

Each pull of his lips had need pulsing hotter between her thighs. She couldn't keep from thrusting against him. She needed so much more. He let go of her nipple with a pop, then grazed his teeth over it, making her whimper.

"What do you want, Muhurua?" he asked her, his eyes locked on hers as he kissed down her belly to stop at her navel. He teased the tender skin of her inner thigh with the tips of his fingers, stroking up and down a few times. She didn't hesitate, spreading her legs wide. She wanted this—him—so much it hurt.

"I want you to touch me," she told him, still holding his gaze.

"Like this?" he asked her as he brought one thick finger down her slit. The caress was soft—too soft. Thrusting her hips forward, she tried to take what she needed, but he shook his head and held her hips to the mattress with his other hand. "I asked you not to move."

"You're driving me crazy. I need you inside me," she whined.

"All you had to do was ask, Muhurua."

His finger was back, and when he stroked it between her folds, Delana closed her eyes and moaned. So good. But she needed more. Before she could ask, he slid his finger up and down again, coating it in her juices before going to her opening. "Look at me," he commanded.

As soon as her eyes popped open, he thrust inside.

He was a big man with big hands. He slid the single digit all the way in, then out again, curling his finger up to stroke her just right. When he pulled out the third time, he paused for a moment, then nipped her lower belly before sliding in a second.

Gasping, she tried to keep still, but the pleasure rushing through her had her arching her back, and a needy whimper drifted past her lips. Already she was close to orgasm, and she had yet to touch him. He bit her belly harder, making her jump, but then he stroked her clit with the pad of his thumb, and the sting was nothing more than an added level of pleasure coursing through her. "Khet, please," she moaned when he did it again.

His hot breath teased at her damp skin, making her nipples pucker. A few inches lower, and she would shatter. He licked his lips again, then stroked the patch of pink skin where he'd bitten her with his tongue. "Are you ready for me to taste you yet, Delana?" The gravelly tone of his voice had her heart racing and her wolf pushing forward.

Her clit throbbed, the pulse centered there making it impossible to concentrate on anything but him as he brought his lips closer and closer. A possessive growl rumbled in his throat as he took a deep breath. Desperate, she tried to thrust upward, but he grinned at her and held her where he wanted her. His hot breath fanned her, and still, he waited.

"Yes, I'm ready. I'm so ready."

With a moan, he lowered his mouth to her. The first stroke of his tongue over her clit had a desperate half-moan, half-sigh rushing past her lips. She wasn't going to last long. He moved the hand he'd held her hips down with around her. Cupping her ass, he pulled her hips higher, giving him all the access he wanted. He growled against her, making her pussy clench around his fingers as he stroked in and out. It was too much, yet not enough. Tunneling her fingers through his hair, she tugged hard, which only had his tongue lashing at her clit faster and harder. His fingers plunged and retreated over and over, each time curling up to stroke that sensitive flesh.

Her legs quivered as she climbed higher and higher. Her moans filled the room, but she didn't care. Just when she thought she couldn't take anything more, Khet grazed the sides of her clit with his teeth, then sucked it between his lips. He didn't go soft or easy. The strong pulls on her clit had her writhing beneath him. Her moans became one long, drawn out cry as the pleasure washed over her, carrying her away.

« CHAPTER 12 »

The sounds of Delana's pleasure echoed in Khet's mind. Her hands still fisted his hair, and the taste of her coated his tongue. It wasn't enough. It would never be enough. He'd intended to give her body release and then leave. But damn if he wasn't too weak—too selfish—to do even that. The beast inside him clamored for release. It wanted Delana with a ferocity that rivaled his own. Khet took another deep breath, inhaling her scent, etching it into his soul. He slowed his fingers, drawing out her pleasure.

"Khet," she gasped as she relaxed into the mattress.

"Tell me to leave, Muhurua. Right now. Tell me to go," he pleaded as he nuzzled her tender flesh.

She lifted her head and looked down at him, her brows drawn, confusion shining in her eyes. "No. I don't want you to go. I want you—all of you." Her voice held all the conviction his spirit did not.

Khet rested his forehead on her lower belly, shoving the beast back. There was no way he would be able to deny her when every part of him wanted her just as much. He would control it. Keep it leashed. Then once he was gone and as far from his mate as he could get, he would give it freedom and let the darkness swallow him whole. It was the only way he'd survive the separation.

When he lifted his head again, she was still looking at him, uncertainty shining in her eyes. He crawled up her body, covering her. Resting his weight on his elbows, he pressed into her. Her breath hitched, then with a glint in her eyes, she reached around him and cupped his ass, giving him a little squeeze before bringing her hands to the front. Her fingers twisted behind the snap. A moment later, she had his pants undone and the zipper all the way down.

Groaning, he waited. She slipped her fingers inside, trying to get them around his girth, but his cock was too full. There was no room behind the denim even for her small hand. He lowered his mouth to hers and moaned when she opened up to him again. So trusting. If only she knew of the monster lurking just below the surface, eating at his soul.

When she couldn't wrap her fingers around him, she pulled at the material of his jeans, tugging at it until it slipped past his ass, and at the front, his cock sprung free. She thrust up against him, and it was all he could do to keep from spreading her open and slamming into her. The beast wanted hard. It wanted fast. It demanded now.

Delana grunted as she used her hands and her feet to get his pants past his knees. The move had her legs open wide, and his cock pressed against her spread pussy, making them both moan. Rather than continue, she left his jeans where they were and wrapped her legs around his waist.

"Now, Khet. Take me," she begged as she rocked against him. She brought her lips to his shoulder, scraping her pointed canines against his flesh. The sensation had need whipping down his spine and into his cock, making it twitch hard.

He couldn't speak as the beast rose to the surface. It's gravelly voice chanting in Khet's mind as it had at the camp. Demanding. *Take. Mate. Mine. Now.*

A growl, much more feminine than his own, tore through Delana. With one hand, she gripped his hair and met his gaze. "Whatever you have, I can take it," she told him before she crushed his lips with hers. Her tongue invaded his mouth. She rubbed her pussy up and down his shaft, taking the pleasure she wanted from him.

With a groan, he lifted his hips, positioned himself, and slid the head of his cock inside. Her channel couldn't take him, it was too tight, but he couldn't stop. He paused for a moment, then pushed in another inch.

"Khet," she moaned, her body tight as she clung to him. She brought her lips to his neck, and again, his cock jerked. One bite. That's all it would take to mark him as hers.

Her fingernails dug into his back, and she gasped when he pushed more inside. He had to stop. He would hurt her, but the beast wouldn't relinquish its hold.

Delana whimpered against him before she opened her mouth and pinched his skin between her teeth. "Now, Khet. All the way," she demanded.

With a groan, he lost the battle and plunged into her. Fire raced through him, making every nerve ending in his body sing. White hot pulses of pleasure shot down his spine and into his cock. He didn't dare move. If he did, he wouldn't be able to stop until he'd taken everything and filled her with his seed.

Her teeth scraped his neck again, and he moaned. The throbbing in his cock intensified until he couldn't think past the pleasure of being inside her body.

The beast's litany grew louder and louder until Khet couldn't hear anything but the sound of its voice in his head. The pounding need of the beast fuelled his own. He pulled his hips back and thrust forward—hard.

Delana's legs tensed around him, but he couldn't stop. He needed to bury himself deep inside her. Mark her so that no other male ever came near her again. His teeth pointed, and before he could stop it, his mouth was poised at her neck. He drove into her, pulled his cock most of the way out, then shoved all the way in.

Her frantic cries drove the beast forward, taking everything she had to give, and still, he could not stop. He slammed into her over and over. Her fingers dug furrows into his shoulders, the pain driving the beast faster.

"Yes, Khet, yes," she moaned as she met his thrusts.

The breathy sound of his name on her lips pushed him past reason. With a groan, he bit down on her neck. The copper taste of her blood on his taste buds had the beast inside him howling. It wanted more. It wanted all of her. He drove harder, deeper, until the muscles gripping his cock trembled and squeezed, shoving him over the edge. Pleasure exploded through him as he filled her with his seed, marking her forever as his. When he released her, he threw his head back and roared.

« CHAPTER 13 »

Khet stood at the village center, waiting. Watching. It had been two days since he'd marked Delana. Two days since he'd allowed himself to see her. He would never forget the hurt in her eyes when he told her he was leaving, but he'd had no choice. The beast had wrested control from him at a time when Delana had been most vulnerable. It was a miracle he hadn't hurt her, or worse. He wouldn't take that chance again.

His spine tingled long before she came into view, yet it hadn't prepared him for the pain in his gut when her gaze roamed over him and then moved on. With her chin tilted up, she crossed the village center to sit with a young male on a blanket in the shade of a huge oak. Fire churned inside him, and he'd taken a few steps toward them when a hand came up, slapping him in the chest.

"You've hurt her enough. I won't let you keep doing it," Joss said as he stepped in front of him.

"Get out of my way."

"Like hell, I will. You're a fucking bastard for marking her and leaving her, and I'd rather die trying to keep you from her than watch you destroy her. She deserves better."

Khet couldn't stop the growl from erupting from his throat. He took a step forward, baring his teeth. The fact that Joss was right didn't matter. That he was her brother was of no consequence. If Joss got in his way, Khet would remove him. Another male was close to Delana, and the beast was furious. Energy sizzled in his right palm, warming his flesh.

Joss's eyes widened, but he stood his ground.

A sharp cough to his right, followed by a deep grunt, were the only things keeping him from using the weapon he'd created in his hand. Wesken glared at him, then growled—not a gentle warning. No, it was all sharp teeth and menace. With a snap of his head, Wesken ordered him to follow.

As soon as they were away from the village center, Wesken had him pinned to the nearest building, his face no more than an inch away. "What the hell do you think you're doing?"

Khet didn't struggle. There was no point. "She's sitting with another male."

"Have you changed your mind?" The man's forearm pressed hard against Khet's windpipe. A human, or even one of the Komoro wolves, wouldn't have survived.

He glared at his pack brother. If he could stay and be the mate she deserved, he would. If he wasn't risking her life just by allowing her near him when the creature inside him demanded freedom every second of every fucking day, then maybe he could think about a future with his mate. But the beast inside him hadn't died as it had for his brothers. The relentless battle for his soul ate what little goodness he had left inside him. And when—not if—the beast succeeded in claiming his very spirit, no one would be safe, least of all, Delana. "No, I haven't changed my mind."

"Then stay the hell away from her," he commanded. "You're the one who denied her. Remember that."

"I'm doing what I have to do to keep her safe."

"You could have done that without marking her. No wolf will take her as a mate now. No Erritrol will look at her. *You* did that. You made sure of it."

"It doesn't matter," Delana's soft voice came from somewhere behind Wesken.

"Delana, please, let me escort you back to the center. I think the feast is about to begin." Even though Wesken spoke to Delana, the hardness in his eyes was all for him. Wesken released him with one last grunt. *Stay away from her.*

Khet wanted to tear into his pack brother for daring to speak to his mate in such a sweet tone. She deserved every bit of sweetness the world had to offer, but Wesken was unmated. And the man wanted to take her away from him. He barely contained the furious howls struggling for release.

"No, thank you. I appreciate the concern, but Khet and I need to talk. Don't we, Muhurua?"

Khet's gaze snapped to hers. "Don't call me that."

"Why not? Would it be better if I called Wesken by that name then? Or one of the other males?" She didn't look at the other man, neither did he, but the gasp coming from the pack's second was enough to have him clenching his jaw tight.

When Wesken stepped aside, she stood there with her arms crossed and her lips turned down in a frown that didn't belong on that beautiful face. *He'd* put that frown there. *He'd* hurt her. Not Wesken, and certainly not that weak male probably still waiting for her in the village center. The pack's second gave him one last, hard look before turning and walking away.

"I have to go," he said more to himself than to her. If he didn't, he'd keep hurting her. He couldn't control the beast anymore. Each time he saw her, it came that much closer to breaking free. His fury turned to ice in his veins. Just looking at her made his chest constrict and his lungs burn for air.

She shook her head but stood her ground. "Why? Why do you have to go? I've made no demands of you. It's obvious you don't want me. I won't force myself on you. I'll even stand by and let you choose another mate if that's what will make you happy," she whispered so softly he barely heard.

"Make me happy? You think another woman could make me happy? The beast inside me has chosen. It was in control when I bit you. If I could take it back, I would. Not so I could take another, but so *you* could be free of *me*. Not the other way around." Khet swallowed around a fist-sized lump in his throat. *She* was fucking perfect. If he were *anyone* else, he would grab hold and never let her go.

"It wouldn't matter. Even if you hadn't bitten me, I'd still be yours. Even if you never touch me again, I will always be yours." Delana's eyes grew bright, and she blinked fast as she turned her head. "The feast is beginning. Since you're so hell-bent on leaving, then at least do me the honor of eating with me before you go."

The resignation in her voice sent a stab of pain through his heart. He wanted to tell her he'd stay, take the tears she tried so hard to hide and make them vanish forever, but he wouldn't lie to her. The sooner he was gone, the better. Come nightfall, he'd be back in the Dark Lands, and the beast would win once and for all.

***

Delana walked back to the village center. She led Khet to a spot near Argram, knowing they would prefer having their men around Miga and Malec this first time attending a social gathering for the new pack. The feast was both a celebration of new beginnings and a welcome to Argram, their new Alpha. Every pack mate would attend. Each would pledge their loyalty to him, which meant each would be close to the toddler and its mother, since they would be at his side.

Between the tight shoulders and the wrinkled brows, he looked like he was ready to explode into action at the least provocation. Joss had told her that Argram and his mate had taken residence in the old Alpha's home, which was as it should be. As far as she could tell, not a single Komoro wolf had objected or complained. But if there was anyone who wanted to challenge him for the Alpha position, this would be when they would do it. None would. But he wouldn't know that.

The Alpha glanced over to where Malec, his son, had stepped a few feet away from Miga to play with a few toys someone had brought for him. He looked at his mate and took a deep breath, only releasing it when she smiled at him.

Hushed voices chattered all around them, but she didn't look at Khet. She didn't speak with him. Until she could do so without making a fool of herself, she would keep waiting, just like the rest of them.

Joss walked up to her, his jaw tightening when he spotted Khet standing with her. He opened his mouth to say something, but she lifted her hand, silencing him. "Khet's leaving after the ceremony and the feast. I've asked him to sit with me for one final meal."

Her brother took a deep breath, then nodded. "Fine. Then let's get this done quickly," he said before going to where Argram stood with his mate standing next to him.

"Argram, as outgoing acting Alpha, in front of my entire pack, I submit to you. I trust that you will lead us well and fairly." With that, he tilted his head to the side, inviting the other man to bite him.

Not a sound rose from anyone around them as Argram performed the necessary task of biting Joss, removing him from his position. The rest of the pack would pledge, but no other bites were needed unless Argram felt the need to show dominance over someone.

Delana stepped forward next. Khet's low growl rumbled between them, but she ignored it. If he had issues, then he could deal with them once he was gone. As the strongest female, the Komoro women looked to her for direction, since they'd had no true Alpha after the last had perished. Seeing her agreement with Joss's decision would go a long way in establishing trust with Argram.

"Argram, I accept your leadership and pledge my loyalty to you and our new pack." Delana tilted her head to the side. She didn't expect a bite, so when his hot breath brushed her neck, she stiffened. Sharp teeth pierced her skin just where Khet had given her his mating bite. Pain shot through her shoulder, and she couldn't help but gasp.

In an instant, a vicious growl came from behind her. Khet stood there, his hands clenched. The wicked sound came again, but another met it. Argram pulled her to the side and stepped forward.

"You wish to challenge me?" Argram's voice deepened as he came nose to nose with Khet.

For an excruciating moment, she thought Khet would say yes. That he would fight his Alpha because he had done what? Dared to bite her as was his right? Her heart pounded. A challenge to the Alpha ended in death—always. *Please, please don't do this.*

Khet glanced over at Miga, who clung to Malec, then over at her, and his gaze fell to the ground. He was silent for several seconds. "I wish no such thing, Argram. I submit to you, as always," he said, even though his voice had turned gravelly and he had his fists clenched at his sides. He then tilted his head, accepting the bite.

When he came back, Khet wouldn't look at her. He wouldn't look at anyone. He just stared at the ground, his shoulders slumped.

The spark of anger that had been festering inside since Khet had left her smoldered and grew. Whatever his issues were, he was letting them get between them. He kept silent as one person after another came forward, pledging their loyalty to Argram. His pack brothers all did the same, renewing their pledges in front of the entire pack.

As Alpha, Argram and his family were served first. Delana stepped forward next. She heaped plenty of meat onto a plate, along with some sweet biscuits one of the omegas had made, and carried the plate to Khet.

"Here. Eat. Since you can't stand the sight of me, you might as well get this done and over with so you can go." Anger laced every one of her words, but she couldn't keep it bottled inside.

When he finally looked at her, the pain in his eyes had her heart stuttering. She didn't want him to go, but things couldn't go on as they were. He took the plate from her. "Thank you."

She sat on the ground next to him, careful not to touch any part of him, though deep inside, she wanted to shake him and demand answers.

He kept his gaze locked onto hers as he grabbed a piece of meat and brought it to her lips. She shook her head, and his jaw clenched, but she wouldn't give in. If he wanted to run, then he had to do it on his own. She wasn't helping him. Not this time.

From the corner of her eye, she spotted Wesken with his plate of food coming to sit between his brother and Khet. Another male did the same, and another. What the hell did they think was going to happen?

"I am not like you. None of us are," he told her as he shoved the piece of meat into his mouth. He chewed slowly and swallowed. "Eating the meat gives power to the beast inside me. It wants more. Always more. It craves it."

Khet broke off another piece, tossing it into his mouth.

"I'm not afraid of you—or your wolf," she told him. And she wasn't. Oh, he'd hurt her plenty, but only by denying her her mate. Physically, he'd been—perfect.

"You should be," he snarled at her. "I'm not kind, Delana. I'm not the right man for you or for anyone else, for that matter."

He shook his head and shoved the half eaten plate of food to the side with a growl. "I'm not even a fucking wolf. None of us are."

Argram growled at him again, but Khet didn't stop. "That thing. In the forest? The one that almost killed you? That was me. I am that beast."

"What are you talking about? You didn't hurt me. I saw it. I saw you," she denied. Memories of bright flashes of light crashed into her mind. It hadn't been him. She'd seen the creature that hit her. But she couldn't deny the memory of the men fighting back with the same kind of energy fire.

"I am not the one who sent that dark energy into you, but that doesn't stop me from being what I am. I am the beast from the forest. I am Erritrol. Not wolf. I will hurt you over and over until there is nothing left of you, and then, I will spit you out. It is the beasts' nature. There is no good inside of me, *Muhurua*," he said with a sneer. "Nothing worth saving."

Her heart pounded as he stood and looked at her one last time. "If I could be what you needed me to be, I would. It's just not possible."

Delana's heart clenched. She wanted to deny it, to argue that he could be what she needed. That he *was*, but he was already walking away.

« CHAPTER 14 »

"Is this true?" Delana rounded on Wesken. She didn't care if he was glowering at her or that she was bordering on insolence. She needed some damned answers, and someone was going to give them to her. What the hell had she gotten her pack into?

When he wouldn't answer, she turned to Argram, but it was Miga who responded. "We are Erritrol, but not as you saw them. Not anymore. What we are today is what we were always meant to be. We are lupine, as you are. A different breed, yes, but lupine, all the same. Centuries ago, our people had allowed the darkness of our land to fill their hearts. As punishment for their wickedness and depravity, our entire species was cursed by the Gods and Goddesses, and we became the creatures you saw in the forest. Not long before we came here, a woman by the name of Brienne risked not only her life but that of her people to break that curse. Because of her, we live again with warmth in our souls and love in our hearts. Khet hasn't accepted that he was one of those saved. I don't think he believes he should have been. Many of our people still live in darkness. It still rules their souls. Those who attacked us in the forest were among them."

Delana turned to Argram again and opened her mouth to speak, but a roaring howl cut through the village. *Khet.* Deep inside, her wolf cried along with him, adding her sorrow. More than anything, she wanted to go after him, but she couldn't. Not with the mistrust shining in the Komoro pack's eyes at the news of a different species in the village. She brought them here. She had to see this through to the end. "Prove it. We need to show the pack that you are, in fact, wolves and that they have nothing to fear." The Erritrols had been in the village for a couple of days, and not once had any harm come to any of the Komoro pack. The Erritrols had taken up residence in the empty homes and had started contributing to the village, hunting with the hunters and providing for the pack. Whether they were a different breed of shifter or not didn't negate any of it, but the pack would have doubts. Only seeing another wolf would assuage that.

Argram stepped forward. "This is the one and only time I will be coerced into doing anything, and I only do this because I wish to do so. I do not want dissension in the pack." Delana didn't have time to say a word before he'd pulled his shirt off. She turned her head while he shucked his jeans.

"You can look now," Miga said, her voice soft and wistful.

When Delana turned to look, a massive gray wolf, larger than any she had ever seen, stood next to Miga. She buried her hand in her mate's scruff, and a soft smile played on her lips. "I haven't seen him in his natural form in days. I've missed him," she said.

The wolf turned to its mate and gave her a long lick on the cheek.

A moment later, Argram lifted his head and growled. Miga reached for Malec, plucking him from the ground where she had lowered him to sit in the grass.

Delana listened and sniffed the air, but nothing other than the smoked meat came through. When she looked around, Wesken was gone, as was Orrin and the other men. Wolves stood in their place, each as big and as menacing as the last. Miga thrust her son into Delana's arms. "Go, take him somewhere safe. Now," Miga yelled as she shifted, tearing the clothing she'd been wearing.

The squirming child cried for its mother, but she was gone. A beautiful black wolf with bright blue eyes stood here Miga had been. All around her, the Komoro pack took the Alpha's lead and shifted.

At once, a familiar, putrid stench filled the village, obliterating the delicious smells of only moments before. It was the same scent that had surrounded her in the forest just before the attack. She whipped her head around, looking for a threat, but she couldn't see anything. Argram growled and took a step toward her, springing her into action.

With the crying baby in her arms, she ran as fast and as hard as she could. If the same beasts were in the village, nowhere was safe. She ran to the edge of the forest and kept running. Branches and briars tore at her bare arms, but she didn't slow down, didn't look back.

Furious howls cut through the forest moments later. Leaves rustled on the trees, and tremors shook the ground at her feet. She wouldn't let Argram down. Gripping the boy tight, she ran. An acidic burn threatened to choke her as bile rose up with the memory of the last battle she'd fought. Her Alpha had entrusted her with the protection of his mate, Rasha. By the time she'd gotten there, it had been too late—Rasha lay in a pool of her own blood, her eyes cold and unseeing. She had died alone and afraid, taking her unborn child with her. Overcome with grief, the Alpha was careless. The wolves attacked. The only reason any of them survived at all was that some of the men who had gone hunting had returned and driven them away.

Delana forced herself to run faster, harder. There was no way she would let any harm come to Malec. They would have to kill her first, and before they could do that, they would have to find her. A small grotto just the other side of the walnut grove would hide them until Argram could come for them. And he would. As soon as the battle ended, he would find his son. Dense shrubs concealed the opening, but she would sneak them into it and wait there.

The tension coiling in her chest eased a little. They were almost there. Another hundred feet, and they'd be safe. She slowed her pace, careful not to trip over any of the roots the last windstorm had brought to the surface. She stopped under one of the walnut trees and held the baby close. He'd stopped crying and was looking up at her, then he waved a chubby fist at her and smiled. They would be okay. She took a deep breath, then another, trying to ease the burning in her lungs, but then stopped short.

Fucking *Mahehkan* wolves. The scent had her muscles tensing. It was too strong to be days old. They had to be close. *Damn it.* She took a shaky step, careful not to make a sound. She couldn't go to the grotto. They would smell her just as she'd scented them, and she and Malec would be trapped. What the hell was she going to do? She took another step. To her right, a twig snapped, then a deep chuckle filled the air.

"Look at what I found traipsing in the forest," a deep voice bellowed from a few feet behind her.

Delana whipped around, her black hair fanning around her to settle like a cloak on her shoulders. Frightened by her sudden move, Malec grasped at her shirt, his chubby little hand pulling at her hair, but he didn't cry.

"Where do you think you're going?" The man asked. Filthy track pants, two sizes too big, hung on his hips, his protruding belly hiding the waistband at the front. He hadn't bothered with a shirt.

"I'm going back to my pack. They're not far. They'll worry if I'm not back there in a minute or two." She took another step, and the man grinned, showing yellowed teeth—what was left of them.

"Is that so?" he asked as he advanced. His eyes shifted to a point behind her, and she groaned. Someone else was there. Rather than look to where he had glanced, she darted in the opposite direction. The one she had spoken to wasn't fit. She could outrun him even if she had just run a few miles to get there. Maybe the other one would be out of shape, too.

Just as she took her first running step, she slammed into a wall of muscle, sending her sprawling to the ground. Malec let out a loud wail. For a second, she thought he was hurt, but he still lay on her chest, his arms and legs flailing in fury, but no tears flowed from his eyes.

She scrambled to sit, but before she could stand, the man she had crashed into grabbed her by the arm and hauled her up. "I don't think she's going anywhere, C.J."

The unkempt man—C.J.—grabbed her other arm. His top lip curled up as he looked at her. "She's the bitch that ran off a couple of days ago. Broke my damned leg, she did. She's gonna have to pay for that." Then without warning, he raised his hand and struck her on the side of her head. Pain shot through her ear, and the trees around her swam in hazy slow motion. When she was finally able to focus her eyes, C.J. already had his arm up again.

"She's not so tough now that she's not with that huge bastard, is she?"

This time, the pain didn't even register as he hit her. The ground came up to meet her. Malec's cry pierced through the forest. She had to stay awake to protect

Malec, but when she rolled onto her side, a big black boot came into view, then all went dark.

« CHAPTER 15 »

Khet controlled his pace as he walked through the village. He didn't look back. Didn't dare glance in Delana's direction. His vision flashed red, and it was all he could do to keep from shifting and rushing back to tear his Alpha's throat out. He made it as far as the forest's edge before throwing his head back and roaring into the heavens. All the pain and fury churning inside him released with the wicked sound of the beast.

Seeing Argram's teeth close over Delana's delicate neck, hearing her gasp, then her small cry when the Alpha's teeth had sunk in had had the beast clamoring for release. Had Argram not bitten in the exact spot he'd given his mating mark, Khet could have dealt with it. But the beast had risen when Argram had all but erased the mating mark he had given her. In an instant, he had been ready to challenge the man who had given him a home within his pack. Ready to kill. Had Miga, Malec, and Delana not been there to witness it, he doubted he would have been able to leash the monster inside him.

Even now, just thinking about it had his fingertips burning as his claws drew to the surface and his jaw aching. His muzzle grew and receded as he fought the shift. He couldn't lose control. Not yet. Not until he'd crossed the portal. Once he was back in the Dark Lands, the beast would shove him aside once and for all. At least there, he wouldn't be harming the innocent, because none were guiltless in his homeland.

Khet didn't slow down until he reached the portal. Chest heaving, he stared into the swirling kaleidoscope. Ten feet. Just a few steps and he'd be as far away from Delana as he could be. She'd be safe. Argram would ensure it. So why did everything in him demand that he turn and go back? An overwhelming need to shift—to run—flooded him. The beast spit and snarled. Not at the world around him, but at *him*. It raked at him, setting his insides on fire. It was more than just its desire to be with its mate. It was an all-encompassing need to get back— to defend. He whipped around, facing the direction he'd come in, and took a deep breath.

The fetid smell of the enemy soured the air. Too lost in his anguish, in his fury, he hadn't paid attention to the world around him. He pitched his ears, trying to hear anything out of the ordinary—sounds from the village—but he was too far. The Erritrols had returned, and he wasn't there to protect his mate. His heart hammered hard. Khet had managed two steps before the beast surged forward. He fell to his hands and knees, and for the first time, he embraced the change. His muzzle stretched long, and his canines protruded. Coarse hair shoved its way through his skin, covering him in a thick, silver coat. Muscles snapped, and cartilage popped.

As soon as it was able to move, the beast bolted, ignoring the deer trails leading back to the village. It leaped over a small stream and bounded over countless fallen trees. Branches whipped at its body, some cutting through its tough hide, but it didn't stop, didn't even slow down. It had to get to her. Had to protect her. He could only hope he wasn't too late.

Blasts of energy whipped through the air around him as he rushed through to the center of the village where he had last seen Delana. Wesken battled two Erritrols, Argram another. Lifeless bodies littered the ground, but he kept going. Joss, in his wolf form, kept just a step ahead of a lesser Erritrol, dodging and circling, tiring it out. Miga, also shifted, stood in front of some of the Komoro women, guarding them. Exertion had nothing to do with the pounding of his heart or the lack of air in his lungs. Delana was gone, and so was Malec.

A huge Erritrol came from around one of the buildings, heading straight for Miga. With a roar, Khet lunged forward, tackling the beast only moments before it reached her. He had its neck within his jaws before the creature had a chance to react. With one mighty shake of his head, the neck snapped. He gave it an extra jerk before letting it fall to the ground at his feet.

Khet backed toward Miga, keeping himself between the enemy and the Alpha's mate. Red energy whizzed past him to crash into the building the Komoro wolves huddled against. They had to get them out of there.

Miga took a few tentative steps away, whining at the she-wolves, pawing at the dirt, encouraging them to trust and follow, but they stayed where they were with their legs tucked between their legs. When another blast shot past him, coming within inches of hitting Miga and getting even closer to one of the females, Khet sprung.

They didn't have time to coax and beg. He circled the small pack and growled, not caring that he sounded as wicked as the creatures attacking the village. A couple of them jumped and yipped while others crouched lower, but he did it again. Better to be afraid than to be dead. It didn't take long for them to scuttle behind Miga. When a beast threw its head back and roared, one of the little females hunkered down again, but he followed right behind, nipping at her flank. With a little yelp, she rushed forward to rejoin the others as they sprinted for the relative safety of the forest around them.

Miga waited until the last one made it past the treeline before shifting. "I entrusted Delana with Malec's safety. Find them. She left the village going east. I tried going after them, but a blast hit me. I won't be able to run fast enough to get to them," she said in a rush. Khet ignored the panic building inside him at seeing the Alpha female's worried look. "At least one Erritrol followed. You have to find them. She got a couple of minute's head start. Hurry."

« CHAPTER 16 »

Ignoring the pain stabbing through her head, Delana forced herself back from the fog in her mind. Something hard and jagged poked at her hip, but she didn't dare move. Opening her eyes, she winced at the sun's glare. Distorted shapes moved before her, and she blinked hard, focusing her gaze. The two men who had captured her had their backs to her. C.J. took a deep drag of his cigarette and then laughed. Whatever they were talking about, they weren't worried about her. She glanced around her as much as she could without moving. Where was she—more importantly, where was Malec?

Off in the distance, she spotted the tall white pine that grew near the edge of the Mattagami River. The tension making her muscles ache eased a little at the sight. She used that same majestic tree as a point of reference all the time when she was out gathering plants. With the sun at her back, she had to be on Komoro land.

She had to figure out how she'd get away from the Mahehkan wolves. But first, she had to find Malec. Delana lifted her head to look around. The moment she did, darkness swarmed her vision, and pain exploded behind her eyes. She swallowed down the bile rising in her throat as her stomach heaved.

Closing her eyes, she took a deep breath, letting the pain wash over her, but before she could do more than fill her lungs, a small, cool hand stroked over her cheek. Heat flared beneath the tiny palm, then trickled into her. The tiny jolt had her gasping. One moment, the pain in her temple flared, the next, it dulled into a throbbing ache. By the time she turned her head to look at Malec, her nausea was gone. He grinned down at her with his pouty little lips, his eyes shining brightly. He placed his palm on her cheek again and gave her another jolt, giggling at her when she gasped again.

Malec twisted so that he faced the treeline. With his chubby arms stretched out in front of him, he opened and closed his fists. "Kt, kt, kt, kt, kt," he said over and over. His little brows furrowed and he craned his neck, trying to find whatever he'd been looking at.

When she looked over, all she saw was a little brown squirrel scurrying from one tree to the next. "Shhh. The kitty is gone. We have to be quiet," she whispered so that only Malec would hear. She glanced over at the men who remained oblivious to her being awake. Good. Let them underestimate her. Let them think they had the upper hand. She'd find a way out of this and get Malec back to his parents.

All she needed to do was get to the treeline two hundred feet away. Once there, she could outrun them. She knew the land. Careful not to make a sound, she rolled onto her back. She'd only have a moment to gather the little guy and take off. But with any luck, by the time they figured out that she was up and bolting, she'd have enough of a head start to make it.

Malec chose that moment to squeal. "Kt, kt, kt, kt, kt…"

The men stopped talking, and her heart sunk. *Damn it.*

"Well, look who's finally awake. I thought we'd have to carry her sorry ass the whole way back," C.J. said as turned to look at her.

Like it or not, this was her best chance. With a quick roll, she gathered Malec and rose. Pain shot through her left arm, but she ignored it. She didn't need it to run.

She only made it a few feet when a tall, towering figure came out of the treeline right where she'd been heading. A black ball swirled in its palm as it glared right at her. It threw its head back and roared.

The pounding footsteps behind her faltered. "What the hell?" She couldn't tell which of the Mahehkan wolves had uttered the words in such a high pitch, but it didn't matter. The creature wasn't after them. It was after her. With one look in the hate-filled eyes, her heart stuttered. It lifted its huge fist and released the energy it had been holding.

Delana lunged left. The shot missed her, but a short, agonized scream told her one of her captors hadn't been so lucky. The smell of charred flesh permeated the area. She was still too far from the forest. The beast roared again, and the ground shook under her feet, making her stumble as the creature took huge pounding steps toward her. A bright flash streaked just above her head as she fell.

She twisted her body, landing on her back to keep from crushing the child. All the air exploded from her lungs on impact, leaving her gasping. She tried to move as the beast closed in, but it was fast. Faster than she would have expected for such a huge creature. The smell of wet fur and fetid swamp assailed her. Malec's eyes grew wide, and he whimpered, tucking his face into her neck as though that would protect him from the monster. She scuttled back, trying to get more space, but it was too late. With yellowed claws extended wide, it rolled a charged ball in its palm again.

"Give the child to me, or you both die," the gravelly voice grated, making her wince.

Delana scurried farther, the sticks and stones tearing at her palms as she crab walked as fast as she could. It wasn't much, but she couldn't give up. "Go back to the hell you came from," she spat at it.

The Erritrol's growl started low in its chest and exploded into a roar that had the earth shaking and the birds in the nearby trees taking flight. It lifted its hand, ready to fire. Her heart pounded. Still clinging to Malec, she rolled. She tucked his body close to keep the beast from reaching the little boy.

She closed her eyes, bracing for the blast, but opened them again when a ferocious growl came at her from the other side. In a flash of silver fur, a massive wolf leaped over her, crashing into the Erritrol. The beast's blast veered off course, hitting the ground a few feet away.

Scrambling to her feet, Delana ran. She didn't stop until she reached the treeline. Malec stiffened and squealed. "Kt, kt, kt." He made his grabby hands gesture toward the fighting beasts.

She ducked behind a large tree, putting the huge pine between them and danger. Khet. What little moisture she had left in her mouth dried. Malec had known what she hadn't.

Delana held the little boy close as she peered around the massive trunk.

Blood oozed from deep gashes in the silver wolf's side. His chest heaved as he struggled to breathe. The beast towered over him, its head thrown back in a roar that had her heart skittering to a halt, then pounding again at the sound. That *thing* was going to kill him. She had to do something.

Delana settled Malec down in the tall grass at the base of the tree. As long as he stayed put, he'd be fine. She didn't waste time stripping, allowing her wolf to shred her clothes as she shifted instead. If she were to have any chance at defeating the beast, she had to surprise it.

When she rounded the tree, her heart stuttered. In the hands of the beast, a massive black charge swirled and snapped. Deep in the pit of her gut, a growl rumbled, louder and louder. She was already upon the creature by the time it heard her coming. She leaped up, clamping her jaws around its meaty forearm. She didn't let go until it stumbled back. The blast shot past her, hitting a tree a short distance away and sending bark missiles exploding through the air.

Then with one jerk of its arm, the Erritrol sent her hurtling the way she'd come. Bones in her back crunched, and pain stabbed through her spine as she crashed into the massive pine. She landed in a heap at its base. Gasping, she tried to get back on her feet, but her legs wouldn't budge.

A bright flash had her closing her eyes before everything went black.

« CHAPTER 17 »

Khet threw every ounce of energy he gathered at the Erritrol. The beast's eyes rounded, and it shimmered as though it meant to return to its world, but it was too late. The blast crashed into it, sizzling with power. The Erritrol fell to its knees, smoke billowing from its mouth in a silent roar. Seconds later, the creature was nothing more than a pile of ash.

He had to get to Delana. Why the hell hadn't she run? Scrambling back onto his paws, he turned in the direction she had been sent flying. Heart pounding, he took a step, then another. The invisible vice around his chest tightened, making it impossible for him to breathe. Where the hell was she? He'd heard her crash. There was no way she was moving on her own. Deep inside, the wolf wanted to howl. It had heard the sickening snap of her delicate bones and the breath wheezing out of her lungs, but Khet refused to believe it she was dead.

Delana was alive, and those bastard Mahehkans had gotten to her while he'd finished off the Erritrol. He could smell every last one of them. A quick look around revealed what he already feared. Malec was gone, too. His growl rumbled through him with every step he took. The forest and everything in his sight flashed in various shades of red. He put his nose to the ground and followed the trail. They only had a couple of minutes on him. They wouldn't get far.

He lost the scent for a moment at the edge of a brook, but with one large leap over it, he picked it up again, stronger than ever. Fiery pain in his right side slowed his pace, and blood clumped the fur around his wounds, but he kept moving.

When he heard the sounds of deep voices just over a hill, he crouched onto his belly and crawled to the top. On the other side, a dozen men stood. Delana lay at their feet. Her eyes were closed, but her cheeks were pink, and her chest rose and fell. Malec sat next to her, tapping her cheek with his little hand as though trying to wake her. The men looked around, their wide eyes darting from one place to the next, the smell of their fear burning at his nostrils.

"What the fuck was that?" the biggest of the bunch asked.

One of the other men jumped when a bird flew off a nearby branch, taking to the sky. "I don't know, but I say we leave the bitch and kid here to die and get back to Mahehkan land. I didn't sign up for that shit."

"We can't leave her. Roger gave us an order," the largest male said. "Besides, if that huge fucking wolf is still alive, she's our only bargaining chip. Now pick her up, and let's get out of here."

When one man bent to pick Malec up, the little cub howled and clamped his teeth onto the man's hand. The man grabbed Malec by the arm, shaking him like a rag doll.

Khet leaped from his spot, landing inches away. With his lips curled back, he snarled his warning. *Hurt the boy, and you die.*

The man dropped Malec, and rather than run as his friends had done, he shifted. Khet took a step closer to the idiot wolf who dared challenge him. The fur on its scruff bristled, but it didn't back down. All around him, growls came from the forest.

When the wolf lunged, mouth open wide, toward Malec, Khet pounced. Khet's beast reveled in the sound of the wolf's neck snapping in its jaws—at the taste of its blood flowing over its tongue. And it wanted more. Another wolf came out, then another, circling. Neither stood a chance against the beast. It needed vengeance. It fed on death. And it wouldn't stop. Not until it destroyed every threat, every enemy.

***

Delana became aware of bursts of heat shooting down her spine. Little hands tapped at her cheeks. Malec. She wanted to haul him into her arms and take him away from the horrendous battle being waged, but her legs refused to budge.

Wicked snarls and growls surrounded them. A yelp and a crash a few feet away had her whipping her head around. Blood sprayed in an arc, landing on her skin—on Malec. She pulled him over her, getting him as far away from the fighting wolves as she could. A flash of silver fur, coated red, sprung past, crashing into another opponent.

The battle only lasted a few minutes, but when it was done, wolf bodies were strewn all around her. Only the silver wolf she knew to be Khet remained.

He came to her then, his head low, his lips still pulled back in a snarl. He sniffed the air then circled her so that she had to crane her neck to see him. So much blood. It dripped from gaping wounds all over his body.

Malec tapped her cheek again, sending another jolt of pain down her spine. Crying out, she tried to grasp the little boy's hand.

Khet was there in an instant, his cold, dark eyes trained on the boy. His growl rumbled deep. His pointed teeth dripped a mix of blood and saliva.

"No, Khet. He's not hurting me," she told him, keeping her voice soft and steady. And he wasn't. Not really. The first jolt down her spine had morphed into a warm tingle after the initial shock had rushed through her. And after what the child had done before, she was convinced he was trying to help her.

The wolf sniffed her neck, then down her side before he whined and sat next to her.

"Kt, kt, kt, kt," Malec whispered and dug his fingers into the wolf's thick fur.

"That's right. Khet's here to help us," she cooed at the child, hoping to soothe the wolf at the same time.

Khet looked at the boy, before laying next to her. One of its long claws scraped against her leg, making her hiss at the long, burning scratch. She gasped a moment later as realization set it. She felt the scratch.

"I think he's healing me. Is that even possible?" she looked at Khet, then back at Malec, who was waving his chubby little fists around.

Khet nudged the boy with his nose, making him giggle before he toppled over. When he righted himself and reached for Delana again, the heat rushed from his little palms, warming her spine once more.

"He is. I know he is," she whispered, but before she could test out her theory and try to move her legs, a huge wolf, bigger than even Khet, leaped into the clearing. Its gray fur rippled over its body as it moved, getting closer with each step it took.

Khet was up and between them in an instant. The hair on his scruff stood on end as he growled and snarled at the intruder.

A moment later, a female came into the clearing. The black wolf strode right up to the larger of the two, nudged it with her nose, and then went over to Khet. She didn't hesitate, not even when he growled louder. When the wolf stopped, she shifted, and Miga stood in her place. "Thank you for saving Malec, Khet," she said, before heading straight for her son.

« CHAPTER 18 »

Delana stood on shaking legs. Khet's arm supported most of her weight. It hurt like hell, but she wasn't about to make a peep. Who knew how little it would take to set the men off again?

After Argram and Miga had stormed the clearing— and upon seeing Malec with his skin covered in blood—it had taken everything Miga had to keep Argram from tearing apart everything in his sights.

Wesken and Joss had followed right behind, and again, the snarling and growling had erupted. Even now, she was sure the only thing keeping the men from shifting was the fact that Malec slept peacefully in his mother's arms.

"I'll take the lead. Joss is at the back," Wesken said, giving Argram a glare that dared him to argue.

When none came, he nodded and started off, expecting the others to follow. Delana took a deep breath. She was able to stand, but until her wolf finished the healing the little guy had started, walking would be next to impossible.

Without warning, Khet swooped her up into his arms. He hissed a breath between his teeth, but set his jaw and took a step.

She wiggled to get free. "No. Stop. Your wounds—"

"I'm carrying you."

"But—"

Khet looked down at her, his brown eyes determined. The growl coming from deep within his chest cut off her argument. He was in control, but not by much.

Rather than fight him and cause him pain, Delana relaxed in his arms, laying her head upon his shoulder. She breathed his scent, took in his strength, and allowed herself to drift into a hazy half-sleep until the sounds of the village roused her again.

A few of Argram's men were directing the others and the Komoro wolves as they extinguished fires and repaired damage all around them.

When Khet turned toward her home, she would have argued, but there was no point. He wasn't ready to hear reason, and nothing would dissuade his purposeful strides. If her instincts proved right, she was about to be tucked into bed.

Before he could reach her front door, Joss opened it. She expected her brother to go inside, but he waited there and let them through.

"You'll stay with her?" her brother asked. "I'll take that as a yes," he muttered under his breath when Khet grunted and kept going.

Khet didn't stop until he had her in the bathroom with the door closed behind them. He set her on her feet, not uttering a word as he turned the faucets and adjusted the temperature as the tub filled. With trembling fingers, he removed her clothing, piece by piece, and then let them drop to the floor at their feet.

Delana pushed the hair out of his eyes. He didn't meet her gaze. The grinding of his teeth and the iron set of his jaw made her ache for him. "Khet," she started.

Delana lifted her hand to the bump on her temple, wincing at the ache throbbing there. She was about to turn to look in the mirror when he grasped her by the shoulders and held her still. He grunted and shook his head. Once he had her naked before him, he scooped her up and set her in the soothing heat.

With a hand on her shoulder, he eased her down until her hair floated in the water around her. He took his time, gently massaging shampoo onto her scalp before rinsing it.

He laid her back, careful not to jostle any part of her before wetting a washcloth and ringing it out. When she lifted her hand to take it from him, he ignored it and swiped the soft material over her forehead. Each gentle stroke on her skin relaxed her a little more until her muscles released their tension and her eyelids grew heavy.

***

Delana closed her eyes, and Khet took a deep breath for the first time in what felt like hours. Every time he rinsed the damned cloth, and the water came back tinted pink, fury rose, making everything within his sight flash red. He bathed every inch of her, making sure that not a speck of dust nor a drop of blood remained on her beautiful skin.

For as long as he lived, he would never forget the sight of her battered body lying so still on the ground. The only thing that had kept the beast from taking complete control had been the slight rise and fall of her chest, proving that she lived. Had she died, nothing would have stopped it from destroying everything in its path. Not only the Mahehkan wolves, but every living thing within its reach.

Oh, he'd made sure each and every single bastard who'd had a hand in harming her had died. His only regret was that the Mahehkan pack's Alpha hadn't been there. He may have defeated the enemy, but there were more of them out there. The beast had reveled in the bloodshed, demanded to hear their agonized howls. It had wanted more—so much more. But its need to care for its mate had been greater. Tending to her wounds had taken precedence.

Already her body was working to heal her injuries, but in her human form, it would take longer, and the healing would not be complete.

"I'm okay. I am," she whispered and brought a wet hand out of the water to brush the hair from his forehead.

"You're not. Not yet, but you will be," he said, his voice gruffer than usual. Without missing a beat, he stood and scooped her out of the tub. "You need to shift to heal."

"I just need rest. I don't know what Malec did to me, but I'm healing fast. I can feel both my legs again. See?" she said as she wiggled her toes.

"Still, you'll heal better in your wolf form. Or is that not the case with your species?" He grabbed the softest towel from the pile next to the tub and patted her dry before picking her up again and heading to her bedroom. Settling her in the center of her bed, he waited.

"It is. But we haven't taken care of your wounds yet," she said with a stubborn tilt to her chin.

Khet hadn't even thought twice about his injuries. If anything, he'd dismissed them as insignificant and forgotten about them. None of his had mattered in the face of a single one of hers.

"If you shift and promise to stay where you are, I will shower and come back and join you," he offered. It didn't matter that he'd planned to do so anyway. He'd already seen Delana's stubborn streak when she'd tried to eat a huge portion of meat back at the camp. Who knew what she'd do to try to take care of him now, and the last thing he wanted was for her to do anything that would jeopardize her healing.

Delana gave him a good long look, making him aware that he had no clothing covering him. Not that he minded her looking, but having her eyes on him only incited the beast closer to the surface again. *Mine. Mate.*

Two days. We will let her heal. Then we can claim her again, he assured the beast. He only hoped that, after what he'd put her through, he wasn't lying.

"I will, but you have to give me something in return."

"And what is that?" whatever it was, if it were in his power to give it, he would.

"I want to know what Muhurua means," she demanded.

He looked at her and damned if his lips didn't want to turn up and smile. "I'll tell you what... Once you've had time to heal, and we've talked, if you still want to know, I will tell you."

She looked at him again, appraising him. "Fine. Don't be long," she told him before shifting.

Khet didn't waste any time. He had no doubt that if he took more than a few minutes, she would get up and come looking for him. But by the time he returned with a pink towel wrapped around his waist and his hair still dripping from the shower, she was fast asleep.

His chest tightened at the sight of his mate. Shifted, he couldn't see the fading bruise on her temple or the angry red lines where claws had raked her back. He could almost pretend he hadn't heard her spine snap when she'd attacked the Erritro to save him. But he had. Only a miracle had saved her. That, and a tiny boy who had more control over his abilities than any of them put together.

Khet took a deep breath, savoring her scent. He hadn't been there to protect her when the enemy had come, but he'd be damned if that would ever happen again. Even if she didn't accept his claim, he would stay in the village and keep her safe. Now he had to pray the Goddess would shine her light upon him again and Delana would forgive him.

« CHAPTER 19 »

Delana stretched and snuggled deeper into Khet. The last time she had woken, she'd glanced at the clock, shocked to find that she'd lost an entire day. She would have gotten up, but her wolf hadn't wanted to move. With Khet so close, it had been more than happy to give him a long lick on the muzzle and go back to sleep. At some point, she'd shifted back to her human form, as had he, and she lay there, wrapped up in him.

With the weight of his arm around her waist and the heat of his chest at her back, she once again had the urge to stay right where she was. Too bad her body wasn't tired anymore. Even though her muscles were tight, the soreness was gone. She gave her toes a reassuring wiggle and moved one leg, then the other before releasing a sigh.

"Feeling better?" Khet asked, his whisper husky as he pulled her tighter against him.

"Much."

He was silent for so long, she might have thought he'd drifted back to sleep, but with each passing second, his body hardened with tension that had nothing to do with the fact that they were both naked and in bed. Whatever he had to say, he'd have to come out and say it. She wasn't going to make it easy for him to tell her he was leaving again.

"I'm sorry. I should never have left. I was a fool."

Delana's breath whooshed out of her lungs. Okay, that was a lot better than what she'd expected. She twisted in his arms to face him and was about to say something when he pressed his lips to hers, silencing her.

"I know I hurt you, but I want you to know that, regardless of your decision, I am not leaving again. I..." he growled and took a deep breath. "I was going to say that I would step aside and let you choose another mate if that was what you wanted after how I treated you, but I can't. It would be a lie. Just the thought of you with another man makes me crazy."

"I don't want another," she told him softly.

He looked at her, his eyes unbelieving. "The beast inside me—"

"Is nothing like the Erritrols that we saw in the forest. Nothing like the ones that attacked the village." She lifted her hand up to his heart, spreading her fingers wide. "You are Erritrol, but you are not as they are."

"I was."

She shook her head. "No, you weren't. Had you been, you still would be. Miga told me about the curse. About how only some of the Erritrols escaped it, and why. You deserved to be saved, Khet. You are not like them. You never were."

"The beast is there, Delana. It fights for freedom. It thrives in blood and death."

He tried to pull his gaze away from hers, but she refused to let him. "It is a part of you, but it doesn't control you."

"But it did. When we were in the forest, it took over. I had no control. I didn't just eliminate the threat, Delana. I slaughtered them. I bathed in their blood. I needed it—craved it. I am no better than any of them."

Her heart ached at the anguish in his tone, the raw pain in the depths of his eyes. He couldn't believe that. She wouldn't let him. "You didn't hurt me. You didn't hurt Malec. You defended and protected us.

And even though you were still struggling when the others arrived, you didn't attack Argram or Miga. You didn't hurt Wesken or Joss, either. Only the enemy. So tell me, had the beast been in control, would it have stopped with the enemy? Would it have stopped as *you* did?"

Khet stared into her eyes. For a moment, she thought he would object again—protest his worthiness. But then he took a deep breath and crushed her in his arms.

Delana breathed him in. There was something in the way he held her which promised acceptance. For him. For her. For the life they would build together. When she pulled back, it wasn't to gaze at him again. No. She wanted to be one with him. To truly be his and to have him be hers. She took his mouth with the certainty that he would be there in the days to come. In the years to come. He was hers, and she wasn't letting go. Not this time.

With a groan, he lifted his hands, tunneling his fingers in her hair, pulling her deeper into the kiss. When he swiped across her bottom lip with his tongue, she didn't resist. Didn't want to. He slid one hand down her back, not stopping until it cupped her ass. With another groan, he pulled her tight against him. There was no question about what he was asking. And there was no way she was refusing.

"I need to claim you again. My wolf needs to claim its mate. Argram's scent on your skin..."

Delana opened her mouth to protest, but Khet shook his head, silencing her.

"I know why he did it, and it had nothing to do with showing his dominance. He was proving a point. To me. He knew what I was too stubborn to face. That I wouldn't be able to live with the idea of you with anyone else. You are my mate, Muhurua," he said as though needing to reinforce the fact.

"You never told me what that means," she reminded.

"My heart," he whispered. "Muhurua translated into English means *my heart.*"

Her lips parted, and she wanted to say something, but the words froze in her chest. *His heart.* All that time, he'd been calling her something so sweet.

When her tongue darted out to wet her lips, his gaze followed. A moment later, he was devouring her. His tongue slipped between her lips, and she opened up to him, eager for his kiss—for his claim. He brought his hand down the back of her thigh to her knee, and with a moan, he lifted it over his hip, spreading her wide open before pressing his hard length against her. By the time he broke the kiss, their breathless little pants mingled. Her heart raced, and heat pooled between her thighs.

"Take me, Khet," she demanded.

"I will never let you go. Not ever again, Delana. You have to be sure this is what you want—that *I* am what you want."

Telling him wouldn't convince the wolf. Hell, it wouldn't convince the man, either. With a quick roll, she pushed him onto his back and straddled him. His big hands slid up her hips, squeezing just enough to make her aware of his strength without hurting. She lifted, reaching between them to grasp his cock at its base.

Khet's chest rose with the breath he took, but he didn't let it go.

Rather than lower herself onto him right away, she slid her hand over him with a long, firm stroke. "You're mine, Khet. All of you," she told him.

The air hissed from between his teeth, but before he could say a word, she positioned herself and came down, taking him all the way in.

Khet's fingers dug into her hips. He moaned and closed his eyes, the muscle in his jaw jerking. "Delana," he whispered, his voice tortured, before opening his eyes again.

"I've made my choice," she told him again. And she would keep telling him until he believed it. "You are mine." She rocked her hips, grinding her clit onto his pelvis. When she lifted, he didn't wait for her to come back down. He thrust fast and hard, filling her.

Gasping, she tossed her head back and moaned. She was already too close. A few more like that, and she would explode. Then again, that wasn't such a bad thing. Later, they could take their time and explore every inch of each other. Right then, she needed to be one with him. She lifted, this time ready for his thrust. When he plunged in again, her toes curled as sensation washed over her. She didn't wait. Digging her fingers into the muscles of his chest, she set a quick tempo, lifting and lowering, then rocking against him. He met each of her downward thrusts with his going up, then pulled her forward when she rubbed against his pelvis. His fingers held her ass so tight she might bruise, but the way he filled her, the way he stroked that sweet spot inside her, she didn't care. She would gladly have his fingerprints on her ass if this were what caused them.

Leaning forward, Delana pressed her lips to his, but when he would have deepened the kiss, she nipped his chin, then kissed along his jaw. She scraped her teeth down the column of his neck. The pulse in her clit throbbed in time with her racing heart.

She gave his skin a little nip, smiling against the pink spot she'd just created when he jumped. His hands, still gripping her ass, pulled her forward, making her moan right along with him.

He knew what she was doing—wanted her to do it, even—but he wouldn't push her along. That was fine by her. She didn't need any urging or convincing, for that matter. There was no doubt for her. The sooner she claimed him, the better.

With an empowered growl, she gave his skin a little lick, then clamped her teeth on his neck just above his right shoulder.

For an instant, neither moved, then with a roar, he thrust up. White hot pleasure streaked through her, filling her, swallowing her. The pulse in her clit exploded as contractions made her pussy clench and release. When she would have lifted her hips to take more, he rolled, taking her with him. She released his neck only to cry out when he pulled back and slammed into her fast and hard.

"Khet," she gasped when he repeated the move over and over. She pulled her hair to the side, exposing her neck. The spot where he'd claimed her tingled, and her nipples pebbled. She needed him to bite her more than she needed her next breath. When he leaned into her, she reached up and pulled him the rest of the way. His hot breath caressed her skin.

With each pounding thrust, she moaned and gripped his shoulders tighter.

Delana pushed her neck onto his mouth, shivering at the feel of his pointed canines. "Please, Khet, now," she begged.

With a half-growl, half-moan, he sank his teeth deep. Crying out, she met his thrusts, their rhythm erratic, yet in sync. Pleasure rushed through her, sending her spiraling out of control. Her fingers dug into his shoulders as her climax crested, sending her soaring. When Khet finally lifted his mouth from her neck, he slammed into her one last time, then stayed there. Throwing his head back, he roared as his cock jerked inside her, filling her.

« EPILOGUE »

Khet couldn't stop touching her. Every inch of Delana's exposed skin was his. What wasn't exposed was his, too. All of her. There wasn't a piece of her that didn't belong to him. And he belonged to her. Every bit of him. He could hardly believe it. Having his mate in his arms, holding her, breathing in her scent, and knowing that nothing short of death would take her away from him had his beast slumbering.

Not long after their mating, peace had stolen over him and had yet to dissipate. That had been a month ago. Delana was the key. She kept the beast at bay with her goodness and her heart. Or maybe the creature was too tired from all the hours they spent making love to dredge up the old hatred. Whatever it was, Khet had never been happier.

The need to escape his mind was still there, but the ever present darkness no longer threatened to steal his soul. He hadn't gone back to the portal since the attacks. He wouldn't have dared, even if he'd felt the need to. The sight of her broken body was etched in his memory and would torment him for all time. He'd never completely forgive himself for not being there to protect her. But *she* had. As incredible as it was, she had forgiven him and given him more than he could have ever hoped for with her love and acceptance alone.

He had to be driving her crazy being underfoot all the time, but she never complained. Khet smiled against her hair and pressed his lips to her temple. He was trying to give her space, but every time he stepped away from her, the beast roused. It didn't like being away from her any more than he did. At least he was hunting again. And eating meat. His stomach growled just thinking of the elk he and Wesken had hunted a few days back.

Delana stroked his chest and sighed. "What are you thinking about?" she asked, her voice sleepy, satiated. He loved that voice.

"You, *Muhurua*" he admitted.

She grinned against his skin. "That's what you always say." She turned her head up, the dreaminess in her eyes making him smile.

"That's because it's true. I'm always thinking about you." He stroked a finger down her back. "About how soft your skin is. How beautiful you are. How lucky I am to have found such a perfect mate. About how much I love you."

She pressed her lips, still puffy from his kisses, to his. "I love you, too, mate."

"If we don't get out of this bed, we will never make it to the feast on time," he told her. And as much as he wanted to keep her home and in bed, Argram would come storming in and drag them to their mating celebration himself if they didn't show up again.

"Worse things have happened. What will they do, start our mating celebration without us?" She nipped his chin, then licked the spot.

"We've already missed it once. Miga will not be pleased if she goes to all that trouble and we miss it again. And if Miga isn't happy..."

"Argram isn't happy." Delana scrambled out of bed. "What time did they say we had to be there?"

Khet glanced at the clock. "In about twenty minutes."

"Crap. Okay." She leaned in and kissed him—hard. "That's to keep you until later," she whispered and scooted out of his reach before he could drag her back to bed.

With his head lowered, he stalked her across the room.

Grinning at him, she pouted her lips at him and gave him a saucy wink.

His soft growl rumbled between them as he took a step closer. "We don't *have* to go."

She held her hands up and backed toward the bathroom, her eyes widening right along with her smile. "You take the guest bathroom. The sooner we get there the sooner we can come back."

"I've changed my mind. I think we should stay in."

Squealing, she dashed into the bathroom and slammed the wooden door, giggling the entire way. "Get ready," she screamed from the other side.

Had Argram not threatened to come after them himself and drag both their naked asses to the feast, he would have followed. Hell, he still wanted to, but it was a special occasion. One that meant a lot to his mate, and so it meant a lot to him.

Once showered, he went into the living room to wait. If he was in the bedroom when she came out, they really might not make it.

His breath caught in his lungs when she emerged a short while later. A pale blue sundress hugged her curves. She had her hair up in a fancy bun with soft curls falling around her shoulders and the gorgeous column of her neck exposed. He'd never seen anyone more stunning.

Khet came to her and took her hands in his. "You take my breath away, Muhurua," he whispered before he pressed a soft kiss to her lips. He didn't know how he ever got so lucky or what he'd done to deserve it, but the Goddesses had smiled down on him when they'd chosen his mate. And he would spend the rest of his life proving he was worthy of this one amazing woman.

http://elianneadams.com/

Follow Élianne Adams

For the most up to date information about new releases subscribe to my Newsletter.

> Online: www.elianneadams.com
> On Facebook: Élianne Adams
> On Twitter: @ÉlianneAdams

I love to hear from readers. If you enjoyed Lost in Magic, please leave a review at Amazon.com or Goodreads.com. Your feedback is invaluable to make the stories what they are.

Élianne Adams

http://elianneadams.com/

About the Author

Born of snow and ice, or at least near snow and ice in North Eastern Ontario, Canada, Élianne Adams has always enjoyed curling up with a good book and a warm blanket. Even before she really knew what love was, she dreamed of writing her own happily ever after stories. It wasn't until her very own hero encouraged her to follow her lifelong dream that she began putting the words begging to be told onto the page. When she isn't reading or writing, Élianne can be found spending time with her husband, three children and pets.